What moms and daughters say about The Broadway Ballplayers™

"This is one of the best books I've read. I learn a lot about sports and life from *The Broadway Ballplayers* books."

—Emily Roth
Basketball player, soccer player, runner, athlete

"Holohan scores again! Angel struggles through complex challenges to emerge a winner."

—Bonny Roth
Mom, coach, sports fan

"Angel and the Ballplayers share sports, secrets, advice, and lots of fun. They face realistic problems and work together to solve them. Through Angel, we learn about dedication, injuries, defeat, victories and passion. This fast reading book keeps you on the edge. I can't wait for the next book in the series."

-Susanna Malarkey
Runner, basketball player, athlete

"An astonishing fresh look at girls and athletics. We watch Angel struggle with today's issues of loyalty, religion, injury, and competition. As a runner I could feel her passion for running and could relate to how she used it to help in other areas of her life. It is the most engaging and realistic book on kids running that I have ever read."

-Mary Ann Malarkey
1994 Chicago Marathon Masters Champion
Coach and mother

"This is a good realistic story about a family and a girl going through a difficult time. This is the way a little girl feels. It is very appropriate for the age group."

—Molly Mullen and Ginny Fitzgerald
Horseback rider/athlete and mother

Other books by **The Broadway Ballplayers™**

The Broadway Ballplayers™

Don't Stop
by Angel

Series by
Maureen Holohan

Printed in the United States of America.
10 9 8 7 6 5 4 3 2 1

For information regarding permission, please write to:

The Broadway Ballplayers, Inc.
P.O. Box 597
Wilmette, IL 60091
(847)-570-4715

Library of Congress Catalog Number:
98-73603
ISBN: 0-9659091-3-1

*This book is dedicated
to those who keep the faith.*

*When you want to give up,
keep holding on.*

Chapter One

God grant me the serenity
to accept the things I cannot change,
the courage to change those things I can,
and the wisdom to know the difference.

When I was in grade school, my mother came home one day and gave me this prayer in a pretty oak frame. After I read the first line, I wanted to ask her what the word serenity meant. But by the time I finished the prayer, I had figured it out.

My mother hung the frame on the wall in my bedroom that same night. I read the prayer almost every night before I went to sleep. Then I switched off the light, whispered good night to my sister, and crawled into my bed. As I stared into the darkness, I made a long list in my mind of all the things in the world I would change. Someday I would raise enough money to build an indoor gym at Anderson Park for all the kids on Broadway Ave. Then I'd find a run-down church and renovate it for people of all religions to celebrate faith and love. I thought of starting an orphanage once, too, but my sister said she thought of the idea first. So I let her keep it.

Then I went to high school, and my dreams disappeared. Between playing soccer and running cross country, I didn't have time to do very much with my friends on Broadway Ave. With my parents constantly arguing, I didn't even want to be around my family. I woke up on a few Sunday mornings and dreaded going to church.

I couldn't talk about how hard this was for me back then. But I will now.

• • • •

"HOLD IT!" Coach Simon screamed madly. Everyone slowed down to a walk. "What are you doing? You're running around like a bunch of fools. Play the game right!"

One player rolled her eyes, and another stood with a hand on her hip. As usual, Coach Simon ranted and raved about how bad we were to the point where nobody listened anymore. It wasn't an issue of our soccer team not knowing what to do. We just had too many people who didn't care. The coach's screaming all the time only made the lazy players care even less.

"WORK, ladies, WORK!" Coach Simon yelled.

I chased down the ball, dribbled it for a while and then kicked a long pass.

"Atta girl, Russomano," she called out to me. "Atta girl!"

I would have preferred if Coach Simon called me Angel or Angela. But she liked calling out last names and talking in military time. I didn't have too much of a problem with Coach Simon except when she cursed. I always forgave her for the swearing and shouting simply because I believed that she cared. She just had a loud way of showing that she did.

"If I don't see some hustle," Coach Simon called out, "we're running!"

Even the lazy players jumped up on their toes. It was no secret that Coach Simon had a history of working players until they couldn't run anymore. I had heard that the athletic director put her on probation after two players fell on their knees and broke down into tears one day at practice. During warm-ups before our games, Coach Simon ordered us through drills and ran us so much that we were out of breath before the game even started. My father always joked that even though we didn't win much, we certainly looked good during warm-ups. I really didn't like it when he said that. I knew he was just kidding, but thinking about our 3-8 record hurt because soccer was my favorite sport, and the season was almost over.

The whistle blew for the final time that day. I waited for the dreaded running call, "On the line, ladies." But Coach Simon didn't say anything. She marched her stocky legs to the center of the field.

"Huddle up!" she called out.

I jogged to midfield. Our coach stood shoulders back, chest out as she waited for my teammates to join us. As Coach Simon began, I looked around. No one even bothered to look at our coach.

"Ladies," she bellowed. "If you don't start paying attention, we're back on that line!"

Everyone stood up straight and stared right at Coach Simon.

"We've got a game to win tomorrow," she continued. "The bus leaves at 15 hundred sharp. Be there."

We huddled up and muttered an unenthusiastic team cheer. I sat down on the ground with a few of the other players and started to stretch.

"Russomano," Coach Simon called out as I untied my cleats, "How far are you running today?"

I looked at my soccer coach and shrugged.

"Tell Coach Kris that I don't want you tired for our game tomorrow," she said.

I nodded even though I knew I would not say a word to Coach Kris, who was my cross-country coach. The idea of running cross-country and playing soccer in the same season didn't go over well with Coach Simon. As the coach of freshman soccer and softball, she made it clear that she was not happy when other sports interfered with hers. I always tried to slip away unnoticed each day after soccer practice, but I rarely made it without hearing a word or two from Coach Simon. It was obvious that Coach Simon saw nothing wrong with running me into the ground during soccer practice, yet she didn't want Coach Kris to do the same.

After Coach Simon walked off the field, my teammates repeated the same things they had said so many times before.

"She's crazy," one muttered.

"Doesn't have a clue," another added.

"She always plays the wrong people at the wrong time," our goalie said.

Our goalie stopped and looked at me. I knew she was waiting for me to say something, but I didn't.

"Isn't she such a pain?" the goalie asked me.

I shrugged. Everyone looked at me.

"Don't you ever say anything bad about anyone?" another girl asked.

I shrugged again and she clicked her tongue. I tried my best not to judge others. If I said that aloud, I knew that most of the offenders around me would think I was pointing fingers and telling them how to live their lives. So I just kept quiet.

"Have you ever talked about anyone behind her back?" one teammate asked.

I nodded and said, "I just don't like to make a habit of it."

"Do you ever think bad things?" another asked. "Even about Coach Simon?"

"I try not to," I said and I sighed in frustration. What my teammates didn't know was that I already had enough on my mind. I had problems bigger than Coach Simon. Soccer may have only been an after-school activity for the other players. But to me, running around on the field was the only time I could put all my fears about my family splitting apart out of my mind.

"Are you going to practice, Angel?" our captain asked.

I nodded my head as I pulled off my hard soccer cleats. I slipped on my soft running shoes. They felt like slippers. But when I stood up and started walking, the pain rushed through the arches of my feet. I winced and started to limp as I walked to the outdoor track. The pain grew less with every step I took.

"See you later," I yelled to my teammates.

"Run an extra mile for me!" our goalie called out.

I smiled and waved. Back in late August, playing two sports at the same time seemed like it would be twice the amount of fun. After two months of tough practices, my back muscles tightened, and my feet throbbed constantly. I promised myself that regardless of how tired I was or how much my feet hurt, I would not stop.

Some days I thought that I wanted to be a doctor and a professional soccer player. Then I would change my mind and wanted to be a lawyer and a triathlete. No matter which occupation I considered, I knew one thing for sure: I wanted to run forever. I loved to run because it was so simple. I thrived on knowing that I could set the ultimate destination and time. I could either follow a beaten path or make one of my own. I pushed away all the hurt and pain and ran with freedom. The harder I ran the easier it was to put all of our family troubles out of my mind.

"I'll be gone for good if that's what you want!"
"How can you be so selfish?"
"You're the one who's being selfish!"

I looked off in the distance behind the track and saw my cross-country teammates line up for their run. Coach Kris held the stop watch in her hand. When I saw my teammates move, I started to jog. I cut across the field and met them halfway. I fell into my usual spot in line, which was behind Trina and in front of Colleen. We took turns pacing our tight group. My body reached a point where it just took over on its own. I kept my steady rhythm and focused my eyes in the distance. Becky's smooth stride led the pack. I caught up and ran next to Trina. Then I looked at Maura. I picked up my pace and Trina stayed right with me. We closed the gap and moved within five feet of Maura. Then we lost our steam for a few seconds and fell back to our usual positions in line. Colleen came up and gave us our second wind. All three of us worked to catch Maura. I glanced past Maura only to see Becky kick the last leg of our run. There was no catching her.

Becky White said in front of all of us once that no one on our team would beat her all year. I took one look at Becky's cocky grin and I didn't care if she was our senior team captain and I was a freshman. I decided at that moment that I was going to be the one to prove her wrong.

When I didn't pass her that afternoon, I felt the frustration growing inside of me. I took a few deep breaths and stared up into the sky. *Be strong, Angel. Don't let her bring you down. Be strong!*

"Medium distance jog," Coach Kris called out. "Let's get started."

Our team started running again. Trina, Colleen and I stuck together and finished behind Maura and Becky for the second time that day. I stared at Becky as I finished. *I will catch you. Just wait and see.*

When all the runners finished, we sat in a circle for our cool-down stretch. I glanced at Becky again and wondered how far she had run before school. Rumor had it that she was so disappointed by her performance at regionals last year that she did double sessions of running before and after school.

"Are we going to have a pasta party for the regional qualifier?" Maura asked.

Coach Kris nodded her head. "Sure," she said. "But where will we have it?"

Everyone looked around. I couldn't possibly have it at my house. Not with my parents behaving the way they were.

"I'll have it at my house," Becky said.

"All right," Coach Kris said. "Two more meets to get ready for the qualifier. We're all going to need to focus on fine-tuning everything, starting now."

My nerves tingled. All I wanted to do was qualify for regionals. That would mean finishing in the top 20 of sectionals. I knew I didn't have a shot at moving on to states, but I just wanted to make regionals. I made it my goal one day, but I didn't tell anyone. Even I knew that qualifying for regionals would be a tough task for a freshman.

Coach Kris finished the details on where our meet would be on Saturday.

"Is there anyone besides Angel who won't be here at practice tomorrow?" she said.

I looked around nervously and wanted so badly to tell everyone why I would be absent. Even though they all knew that I had a soccer game, I always felt bad for missing practice. When no one raised their hand, Coach Kris finished her talk. I unlaced my shoes and rubbed the bottoms of my burning feet.

"How are your feet, Angel?" Coach Kris asked.

"Fine," I said nervously. I stuck my feet back into my shoes and started to tie them up.

"They're not bothering you at all?" she asked.

I shook my head. "They feel a lot better."

"They bother me," Trina called out.

Coach Kris turned to Trina and asked, "Your feet hurt, too?"

"No," Trina said. "Angel's feet stink. That's what's bothering me."

I laughed and so did Colleen. Coach Kris shook her head and walked off the field. After such a long afternoon, it felt good to laugh and joke around with my teammates.

"Finish your stretching," Coach Kris said with a smile, "And go on home."

Then my smile went away. I started to bite my nails. For the past two hours, I hadn't been thinking about going home. I had run the fears right out of my mind. I didn't want to hear them argue. I didn't want to see my little brother Gabe run to his room.

I didn't want to go home. I wanted to stay at practice and run forever.

Chapter Two

After practice, I stood in front of the mirror in the locker room and brushed my sweaty hair. When I heard footsteps behind me, I looked in the corner of the mirror and saw someone walk into the bathroom. It was Becky. She grabbed a paper towel. My mind raced trying to think of something really cool to say.

"Later, Angel," Becky muttered as she hustled out of the bathroom.

I hesitated and then yelled, "BYE!"

I sounded like a complete dork. I should have just muttered a cool "yep" or "later." I shook my head and then looked back at the mirror. I continued to brush my straight hair, which was a habit I had developed in seventh grade. My friends from Broadway Ave. always made fun of my brushing my hair so much, but I didn't care. After a few minutes, I tied my thick hair with a rubber band and then added a blue ribbon. I thought of my sister Faith's asking me about my bows on my first day of high school.

"Angel," she said politely. "Are you going to wear a bow today?"

I looked up from my bowl of cereal and eyed her suspiciously.

"Yes," I said. "Why?"

Faith shrugged and said, "Most kids in high school don't wear bows."

"So?" I asked. I stared at my sister in disbelief. "Will I embarrass you if I do?"

"No," she said. "I was just wondering."

"I think they look nice," my mother told me. "Keep wearing them, honey." When I wore my favorite blue and white ribbon to school that day, Faith never brought up the subject again.

I walked out the back door and onto the pool deck. I looked at the rows of swimmers and picked out my sister right away. Faith's strong kick and smooth stroke always stood out among the others in the pool.

"Keep working, Faith!" her coach yelled. "Nice job."

During her sophomore year, my sister's relay team finished third in the state. I knew this year that Faith's goals were to win the state medley relay and the individual 200 meter butterfly. I wanted my sister to win because she practiced both before and after school. During our Bible study on Wednesday nights, I heard a few kids pray aloud for God to help them win games and events. As much as I was tempted to ask God to give Faith a victory, I didn't. I figured if God was rooting for me or Faith, then it might mean that He was rooting against someone else. I didn't think God kept score like that. There were a few times when I was tempted to ask God for a little extra power, but I knew I already had it in me. I just had to dig deep and find it.

"In both victory and defeat," my father preached, "always remember to carry yourself with dignity and respect."

The whistle shrieked and all the swimmers finished their laps. They picked their heads up out of the water and looked at their coach who stood on the deck above them.

"Cool down," he said. "We're done for the day."

I sat down on a bench and watched my sister move smoothly through the water. I didn't know how she did it. I couldn't stare at the bottom of the pool for more than 30 minutes. I needed to feel myself sweating. I had to see what was in front of me. I'd pick one point and then seek another destination. Picking those points kept me running. I don't know what kind of mind games Faith played to keep herself swimming. I could hold my own with her in everything except swimming. Faith and I sometimes had arm-wrestling and push-up contests before we went to bed. Faith's strong shoulders always overpowered me in the arm wrestling, but I always did more push-ups. We also had contests to see who could paint their nails the best. Our eight-year-old brother, Gabe, was the judge. I always tried to bribe him with treats and money, but he was too smart to allow me to get away with it. One day I offered him a pack of gum, three lollipops and a crisp one dollar bill. I handed it to him and he shook his head.

"Why not?" I asked.

"Faith offered me more," Gabe said.

I was convinced that he had to be bluffing.

"You're lying," I said.

"No, I am not!" Gabe called out loudly.

"Shhh," I said and I looked to our door. "Don't let Mom or Dad hear."

We all knew it wasn't in our best interests if our parents heard us betting or arguing over anything. We were supposed to be the perfect peaceful and loving family. But I had my doubts if there was such a thing.

Faith half-smiled as she walked by me and to the locker room.

"I'll be out in a minute," she said.

I nodded and smiled. As I pushed through the crowded hallways in school and worried about my tests and practice, it always felt good to see my sister even if it was only for a brief few seconds. I think Faith felt the same about me except when I was wearing her clothes without permission. She didn't speak to me for three days after I wore her favorite sweater during the first week of school.

After the entire swim team walked into the locker room, I thought about sticking my sore feet in the water just for a few minutes. Then I wondered how Faith and the other swimmers would feel if I put my sweaty, smelly feet in their pool. So I reached in my backpack and pulled out a textbook. I read until my sister came back out of the locker room.

"Ready?" she asked.

I nodded as I picked up my bags. We walked out the back door of the school with Faith's friend, Kristin, who gave us a ride home almost every day.

"Are you going to the dance this weekend?" Kristin asked Faith.

"Yeah," Faith said and she began to nervously twist her hands. My father set a rule that we could not date until our junior year in high school, which meant the dance would be Faith's first official date. Ever since the beginning of eighth grade, I started to pay more attention to boys and really wanted to start dating. For a while, I took extra time in the morning with my hair and picking out my clothes. I don't know why I did this. My father would have grounded me until I was 25 if he caught me sneaking around with boys. But as my parents started to argue more and more, I lost my curiosity about relationships. I looked at my sister and wondered if she thought about our parents as much as I did.

"How was practice?" Faith turned and asked me.

"Good," I said as I continued to stare out the window.

"Is anybody ever going to beat Becky?" Kristin asked. "All I hear about is how good she is. I hear she goes around telling people nobody can beat her. Is that true?" I shrugged. I was a freshman, but not a stupid freshman. Talking about our captain would not have been the brightest thing in the world. "She's good," I said.

It wasn't as though Becky bragged all the time. One day Maura stayed on her heels during a five-mile run. At the end of the workout, Becky looked at Maura and said, "Nice try." When I heard these words, I wanted to be the one to run past Becky White.

We climbed into the car and drove off. As we turned down Broadway Ave. and came closer to Anderson Park, I saw my friends out on the courts. I then looked to the swing sets and saw my brother.

"There's Gabe," I said. "Could you let me out here?"

Kristin pulled the car over and I glanced nervously at Faith. We both didn't like it when Gabe

20

walked down to the park all by himself. With us being so busy after school every day, we couldn't take him as much as he wanted.

"Will you take my bags in?" I asked. Faith nodded and I jumped out of the car. I ran across the playing field and stopped in front of the swing sets.

"Angel!" my brother called out. He ran up and gave me a hug. I smiled down at his rosy cheeks and runny nose. I reached in my pocket and pulled out a tissue. Gabe turned his head when I went to wipe his nose. He raised his sleeve and swiped it across his face. I shook my head.

"What are you up to?" I asked.

"I'm playing with my friends," he said.

"I don't like it when you come down here alone," I said.

He threw his palms up, stretched his arms out, and looked all around the park.

"I'm not alone," he said. "Look at all the people around me."

"We've got to get going soon," I said.

He looked away from me and whined, "I don't want to go home."

I sighed. I didn't want to go home either. I could hear my parents arguing in my mind.

"Why don't you listen to me?"

"You never listen to me."

"You don't even care anymore."

"You're the one ruining our family!"

"ANGEL!" a voice called out. I snapped out of my daze, turned and saw Molly wave me over. "Come over and take Mike's place."

I looked back at my brother and said, "We're leaving when the game's over. OK?"

He nodded and I jogged off to meet my friends. Wil stood with her hand on her hip. Rosie's blue baseball cap matched the sleeves of her long blue and white baseball shirt. Mud covered the knees of Molly's baggy sweat pants. Penny, as clean and as cool as ever, stood in her matching headbands and sweatbands. She dribbled the ball smoothly around her back and between her legs.

"You're playing with Molly and Wil," Penny said. "The score is 13 up. We're playing 15 straight."

I took my position on defense. I loved to play ball with my friends from Broadway Ave. On the first day we moved onto the street, I dribbled my soccer ball down to the park and met four girls who were playing on the basketball court.

"What's your name?" Penny asked.

"I'm Angela," I said. "But my family calls me Angel."

"OK, Angel," Penny said. "I'm Penny."

The rest of the girls introduced themselves. Then Molly, a red-haired girl with a freckled nose looked at me and said, "You wanna play?'

"Sure," I said.

My new life on Broadway Ave. officially began that day at Anderson Park. We practically lived at the park almost every day after school and for hours on end in the summer. For a long time, outsiders called us the kids from Broadway. That all changed when we chose our full team name for a summer basketball league. Kids from around the city thought our team name was so cool, that even the boys on our block wanted to be called **The Broadway Ballplayers.**

"Ball is in," Penny said and she checked the ball to me.

"Let's end this!," said Jeffrey "J.J." Jasper, who was one of the regulars down at the park. He caught Penny's pass and started dribbling around. I watched carefully as he focused his eyes on Molly, who was one feisty defender. She swatted at the ball as she shuffled her feet. When she banged J.J.'s arm, he didn't call the foul. I left Penny and ran over to double team J.J. He tried to throw the ball to Penny, but I reached up and knocked it away. Then I scooped up the ball and passed it to Molly. She passed the ball to Wil. I cut to the basket and Wil fired the ball at me. I reached up and the ball stuck solidly in my hands. I froze for a brief second as I remembered that I hadn't touched a basketball in weeks.

"Shoot!" Molly yelled. I looked up at the hoop and banged the ball against the backboard. After realizing how badly I missed, I frantically tracked down the rebound. My hands gripped the ball again and I took another shot. I hit the corner of the square more softly this time, and the ball fell right through the net.

"You GO, Angel-cake!" Wil cheered.

I reached out and coolly gave her five. Molly quietly checked the ball to J.J. With the game on the line, players started to cut more quickly, push harder and breath more heavily. I tried to get open, but I couldn't shake Penny off me. When Molly forced the pass to me, Penny stole the ball and scored. Molly apologized to me and then shook her head as she looked up into the sky. "Come on, Molly!" she yelled at herself.

Nobody was harder on Molly O'Malley than Molly herself. But all the yelling in the world would not have changed the outcome of our game. As usual Penny Harris took over the game so quickly that most of us didn't want to believe that it was over. Within seconds, J.J. checked the ball in and Penny scored again on the next play. Game over. That was it. Molly stomped off to the water fountain. I picked up the ball and took a few shots just to cool off.

Penny picked up one of my rebounds and asked, "How's high school, Angel?"

"Good," I said.

Wil hustled back from the water fountain and said proudly, "Did you hear about the fort?"

"What fort?" I asked.

"Mr. O'Malley built it in the backyard," Wil said.

"Yeah," Rosie added. "It's cool."

"We're meeting every Friday night starting this week," Molly said as she jogged back onto the court. "Are you gonna be there?"

"I've got a soccer game," I said. I stared at the ground. I missed hanging out with my friends, who were all still in grade school. "I can come by after it's over."

"The meeting starts at seven," Wil said.

Wil glanced at her watch and shrieked. "It's late! I gotta get going."

"Me, too," Molly said.

We rounded up our brothers and sisters, ran and then we hustled up Woodside. My friends joked around, but I couldn't hear their laughter. All I could think about was not wanting to go home.

"What's the matter?" Penny asked. "Are you all right?"

When I looked up, I realized that she was talking to me. I straightened myself up and tried to smile.

24

"Yeah," I said nervously. "I'm just tired."

"Are you sure you're all right?" Wil said.

I felt my face get hot. "I'm fine," I said firmly.

I looked at Wil and forced out a smile. Wil stared back at me from behind her glasses and her eyes narrowed.

"What?" I asked defensively.

She tilted her head and raised her eyebrows at me.

"Why are you looking at me like that?" I shot back.

"No particular reason," she said with a sly grin. "Just checking things out."

"Checking what out?" I asked.

"Now that you're in high school, I just want to make sure you don't think you're too cool to hang out with grade school dorks like us."

"I'm no dork!" Molly said.

"Yeah, you are," Wil said. "Nobody told you?"

We all laughed at Wil, who was one of the funniest and smartest people I'd ever met. Wil was the favorite to win the city's Brightest Stars competition which was coming up in a few weeks and she was studying like crazy.

"I've got to win," she told me. "This is so big for my career."

"You're only in eighth grade," I said.

"This is just the beginning," she said. "I'm going to be President someday. I'm going to make laws giving women more rights than men. Then we'll see how they feel!"

"You got my vote," I told her with a smile.

What amazed me about Wil was how much she made people laugh even though her life was so difficult. Wil's mother had died before I arrived on

Broadway Ave. From what I had heard from the rest of the Ballplayers, Wil never talked about her mother's passing, and no one ever saw her cry about it either. On the one-year anniversary of her mother's death, I asked Wil if she wanted to go to church with me. She shook her head and said, "I go with my grandma two or three times a year. But don't worry about me, Angel-cake. God knows me. We're on a first name basis."

Before half of us turned our separate ways that day, Wil called out, "Don't forget about the fort tomorrow night!"

We waved and then turned and walked down the street.

"When are cross-country regionals?" Penny asked.

"Two weeks," I said.

"How are your dawgs?" Penny asked.

The Ballplayers called my feet "dawgs," which always made me laugh. I grinned and said with a smile, "I'm struggling."

Penny knew I was half-joking and half-serious. Unlike when I was around my high school teammates, I did not hesitate to complain about my feet around the Ballplayers.

"Take care of 'em," Penny said as she jogged up her sidewalk. She turned back to me as she kept backpedaling. "We need you at the park."

Penny smoothly spun around and bounced up her steps. Her little brother Sammy followed right behind. Gabe and I both yelled good-bye. As we walked further down Broadway Ave., my brother stared blankly at the ground.

"How's school?" I asked.

"Good," he said.

"Do you have any homework?"

"I finished it," he said.

We walked down the sidewalk next to my brick house. I turned the handle of the back door and let Gabe in first. My mother stood over the stove stirring a pot of pasta.

"Where have you been?" she asked as she stared at my brother.

"At the park," I answered for him.

"I wish you wouldn't go running off like that," she said.

"I told you where I was going," Gabe said.

"No, you didn't," she said. "You shouldn't be out so late. I'll have to talk about this with your father later. Maybe he can talk some sense into you."

I could tell by the lines under my mother's dark eyes that she hadn't slept in a long time. She spent her days as a teacher's aide for a third grade class in one of the toughest schools in the city. Up until the last few months, she had always tried her best to stay positive even with her mind filled with worry about her students, who had difficult lives at home.

"I'm hungry," Gabe said.

"Dinner will be on the table in 30 minutes."

"Will Dad be home soon?" Gabe asked.

"I don't know," she mumbled.

My parents tried their best not to talk badly about each other in front of us and in public. But the thin walls in our house allowed us to hear every-thing.

"If you are so unhappy, why don't you go?"

"Do you want me to leave?"

I walked into my room, said hi to my sister, and tossed my backpack on my bed. Gabe peeked in

27

our doorway and asked, "Can you help me with my homework?"

"You told me that you finished it already," I said.

"I forgot about one thing," he said.

"Hurry up and go get it so we can finish it before dinner."

Faith was sitting at the desk. "You don't need to use the desk tonight, do you?" she asked.

I shook my head. "I've got a lot of reading to do."

I sat down on the floor and rested my back against my bed. I flipped open my book and began to read. My brother ran in and set his papers down in front of me. I started to quiz him on his spelling words. At first, he made a lot of mistakes, but within five minutes he knew how to spell every word correctly.

"Are you sure that you still need to study these words?" I asked suspiciously.

"Yes," he said. "I want to get an A plus."

I went down the list one more time and he spelled every word perfectly. I smiled at my brother. But when he wasn't looking, I rolled my eyes and looked at Faith. It was obvious that Gabe did this just so he could study in the same room with us.

A few minutes later, I heard the front door open, and then my father's deep voice muttering something to my mother. Within minutes, the voices grew louder and clearer.

"I had a lot of work to do," he said. "I can't get home any sooner."

"I need some more help around here," she said. "That's all I'm asking."

I heard my mother's footsteps come down the hallway. "Dinner is ready," she said pleasantly.

One by one, we organized our papers and books, and left the bedroom. I reminded myself to be strong. *This will all go away. Things will work out.*

"Hi, kids," my dad said. "How was your day?"

"Good," I said. He walked over and gave us each a kiss on the cheek.

We all washed our hands and then Gabe and I finished setting the table. Then we all sat down and my father led us in prayer. It felt so good to pray together. I missed praying together as a family. We used to be able to stop everything, clear our minds and be together. I looked around the table and noticed that we seemed like a normal family. Our mother and father both came home from work. The kids worked on their homework and helped get ready for dinner. Our parents sat at each end of the table and we said grace. Everyone asked politely to pass bowls and dishes. Normal families like ours weren't supposed to have problems. Then I stopped and asked myself a difficult question. *What is normal?*

The ringing of our phone ended the peacefulness. My mother huffed. I crossed my fingers and hoped it wasn't for me.

"I should have taken it off the hook," she said.

Faith stood up and answered it. "Just a minute please," Faith said and she handed my father the receiver.

My mother huffed again as my father began speaking. He set the phone down and went into the living room. "Hang it up, please!" he yelled.

I tried making small talk just to keep my mother's mind off her thoughts about my father's leaving the dinner table. We all knew what the phone call

29

was about. My father and one of his friends at church decided to start their own ministry on the East Side of the city. After working all day, my father usually went into his own little office in the house and continued on his project until late in the night.

A few minutes passed and my father returned to the table. No one said a word.

"I've got a soccer game tomorrow," I said.

"I know," my father said. "I'm going to try to be there."

Another second of silence passed.

"It's Friday," my mother said. "Please take a few hours off."

"There's so much to do," he said. "I've got a stack of applications to fill out for grants and funds."

"I'd just like it if you could be around a little more," my mother said.

"What?" my father said. "Do you think I like not being around?"

"No," she said. "I didn't say that."

"I'm trying to do something good here, and you're not supporting me," he said. "Why not?"

"That's not true!" she shouted.

"Stop yelling!" he shot back.

"I'm not yelling," she said. "You just don't listen."

I felt the tightness in my face and the tears in my eyes. *Why did I have to bring up the soccer game?* The harshness of their words made me cringe. When I looked across the table at my little brother and saw his tear-filled eyes, I dropped my fork and knife. They clanged against my plate. I stood up and pushed back my chair. It screeched against the floor as I jumped up and headed for the door.

Chapter Three

"**A**ngel!" my father shouted. "Come back here!"

I gripped the handle of the door and turned back to the table. "Why do you have to fight so much?" I pleaded. My voice cracked as the tears poured out of me.

"Please come back and sit down, Angel," my mother said firmly.

I flung open the door, stepped outside and slammed it shut. I sprinted down the steps and starting running as fast as I could. I pumped my arms and sucked in the cold air as I ran wildly through the darkness. After feeling so weak and helpless at the kitchen table, I felt strong. Then the warm tears started to stream down my face as the unanswered questions raced in my mind. *Why are they doing this to us? Why can't they get along?* I turned down Woodside and headed for the park. I looked in the distance and saw no one. I locked my eyes on the park bench and sprinted to it. Then I focused on the basketball court and ran until I reached it. I looked at the backstop on the baseball field. I pivoted and moved full steam ahead.

After about an hour, my mind flashed back to the scene I had left. *What about Gabe and Faith?* I had left them behind. *How could I be so selfish?* I backtracked across the park, up Woodside, down Broadway and headed back to our house.

When I reached our driveway, I walked slowly down the sidewalk. I folded my arms across my chest as I stood at the back door. I took three deep breaths before I turned the cold brass knob. I gave the heavy door a push with my hip and opened it just enough for me to slip inside. I slowly shut it until I heard the lock click. I tiptoed up the back steps and then turned the corner. My eyes stopped at the sight of my father sitting in his chair. He looked up at me and waited for me to explain myself. I refused to apologize.

"Where's Gabe?" I asked.

"In his room," he said.

I walked toward the hallway and mumbled, "Good night."

"Angel," my father's voice rose. I slowed to a standstill. "I'd like to talk to you for a minute."

I turned around, looked up from across the room, and waited for him to begin.

"Come here and sit down," he said.

I walked into the living room and sank down on the couch.

"Your mother and I are having a difficult time right now," he began. *What do you mean by difficult? How difficult? Will this difficult time ever end?*

"I don't want you to let it affect you or your brother and sister," he added.

I looked away from him, thinking of how impossible it was for him to think we could do such a thing.

"You have to be strong," he said. "Don't let this tear you apart."

I had listened to my father speak in front of crowds of people with the most beautiful, moving words I had ever heard. But the man who sat across from me suddenly became a stranger. Nothing he said could give me comfort. The way he and my mother acted went against everything he preached. I had nothing else to say. Nothing made sense. It felt like a nightmare. I muttered good night and walked quickly down the hallway.

"Angel," I heard a voice whisper.

It was coming from Gabe's room. The lights were off and the door was cracked open. I quietly pushed the door open, walked in and sat down beside him on the bed. With the lights off, Gabe couldn't see my red eyes.

"I'm afraid, Angel," he said. "What is going to happen to Mom and Dad? What is going to happen to us?"

I bent over and gave him a kiss.

"Everything is going to be all right," I told him. "You've got to have faith that things will work out."

That is what we learned in church. That was also what my father and mother told us. But I wasn't sure what to believe anymore.

I walked into our bedroom and saw Faith asleep in her school clothes with the lights on. I turned off the overhead light and flicked on my night light and tried to read a textbook. I set it down and worked on my math homework for a few minutes. Then I tried to read again, but I couldn't concentrate. I reached into my night stand and moved my hand around until I felt the Bible with my fingertips. I gently lifted it out of the drawer and opened it to the book mark. After a few minutes, I couldn't keep my eyes open. I fell fast asleep.

• • • •

When I woke up the next morning, Faith was gone. I didn't even hear her get ready for swim practice. I sat up on my bed and hung my legs over the edge. I shifted my weight onto my bare feet, stood up and felt bolts of pain through my feet. I fell back down on my bed. My heart started to pound. All I could think about were regionals being two weeks away. I stood up again and took one step. Then two. I limped into the bathroom, turned the faucet and put my feet in the tub. The hot water made all the pain disappear.

After my shower I went into the kitchen. My mother had a plate of warm muffins waiting for us.

"Good morning," she said with a smile.

I sat down next to Gabe and read a box of cereal as I ate my muffins. My father walked into the kitchen holding a cup of coffee in his hand. He rubbed my brother's head and said good morning to all of us. Then he left for the shower. I looked around amazed at how much things had changed from the night before. Nothing made sense.

"What time is your game today, Angel?" my mother asked.

"Four o'clock," I said.

"I'll be there," she added.

I finished breakfast and then packed my bag for school. After saying good-bye to my mother, I walked Gabe down the street to the bus stop.

"Don't worry about Mom and Dad," I told him again. "Things will work out."

He nodded his head, but his downcast eyes told me that he wasn't quite convinced of my promise.

He waited with the other kids on the corner. I turned and continued down Broadway Ave.

I stood silently as I waited for the school bus with some older kids. I missed going to school with the Ballplayers and couldn't wait until they were in high school with me. Within five minutes, the bus pulled up and I climbed up the steps. I spotted Trina and Colleen and sat down next to them.

"Hi, Angel," Colleen said.

Then a few soccer players got on the bus. Our goalie sat down in front of me.

"Hey Angel," she said. "Are you coming to the party tonight after the game?"

"What party?" I asked.

"Hannah's," she said. "The whole class is going to be there."

Then I remembered about my promise to meet the Ballplayers.

"I'm hanging out with a few of my friends from my street," I said.

"You can't miss this party," she said and her eyes grew wide. "Everyone is going to be there."

I looked at our goalie and wished she would get this excited about our soccer games. She turned to Trina and Colleen. "Are you two going?"

"For a little while," Trina said. "We've got a meet tomorrow, so I'm not staying late."

The goalie then turned to me again. "Come on, Angel," she said. "You never come to the parties. Why not?"

I shrugged. "I promised my friends that I'd hang out with them tonight," I explained.

I never understood what the big deal was about going to these parties. I went to a few in eighth

The Broadway Ballplayers™

grade that I really didn't like, and I heard in high school they only became worse. I would rather hang out and play ball at the park than be with a bunch of drunk high school kids smoking the night away. What was fun for some people just wasn't enjoyable for me. I had promised the Ballplayers that I'd be at the fort, and I was going to stick to my word.

When we arrived at school, I made a long list of all the homework I didn't complete the night before. Fortunately I had a late morning study hall to catch up on my assignments. As I rushed off to class, I saw Coach Kris walking down the corridor.

"Hi, Angel," she said. "Are you ready for the meet tomorrow?"

I nodded and smiled.

"Two weeks from tomorrow, and regionals are here," she reminded me.

I nodded again and hustled down the hallway. I turned the corner and almost ran into someone. It was Becky.

"Sorry," I blurted out.

"That's all right," she said. "Save some of that energy for tomorrow and maybe you can keep up with me."

She walked passed me with a grin. "Good luck in your soccer game," she added.

I stood still, unable to believe what she had just said. *I'll keep up with you all right. You wait and see.* I hustled off to class, wanting so badly to tell Trina and Colleen about Becky's conceited words. But as I sat in class, I thought everything through again. Maybe she just said that to encourage me. After all, she did wish me luck in my soccer game. *Did she always mean to sound so arrogant? Did she think that I could keep up with her? Did she really care if I did?*

I thought about Becky for a while. Throughout the day I was tempted to open my mouth and tell the story about Becky, but I didn't. I reminded myself that I was a smart freshman and decided not to tell Trina and Colleen. After school I hustled down to the locker room and dressed for our soccer game. My nerves tingled and I felt butterflies in my stomach as I tied my cleats. I didn't think about our record at all. I just couldn't wait to play.

"Is everybody going to the party tonight?" our center-forward called out.

I shook my head. *Doesn't anyone care about our season?* Coach Simon burst through the door of the locker room, and all talk ceased. "Let's go, ladies! We've got a game to win!"

When she left, everyone continued to laugh and joke around. I hurried out onto the field so I could warm up my feet. After a few minutes of stretching, my feet felt normal. I hoped they would stay that way, but I just never knew when the pain would sneak up on me again. As I stretched, I looked over and saw my dad's car pull into the parking lot. I smiled thinking of all the work he had to do. I stared into the sky as I stretched and thought of how thankful I was that my father took time out to see me play.

"Come on, Russomano," Coach Simon called out. "Let's go!"

I eagerly stood up, kicked the ball back and forth and jogged around. The rest of my teammates took the field and we began our official warm-ups with Coach Simon taking us through all the fancy drills.

I peeked up for a moment and looked through the crowd. My mother still hadn't arrived. *Where is she?*

"Work, Russomano, work!" Coach Simon said.

"Everyone must do what Simon says," my teammate muttered sarcastically.

When the game started, I worked as hard as I could through the first half. Even with the nine other players out there with me, I felt alone. No one put in any extra effort. No one played hard. At half-time, Coach Simon let us have it.

"Where are your heads out there?" she asked. "All you're thinking about is this party tonight!"

There was a long pause.

"What time is the party?" our coach asked.

No one replied.

"I said, what time is the party?" she asked again. "Somebody answer me!"

"Seven o'clock," a player called out.

Coach Simon scribbled something down on her dry erase board.

"Where is it?" Coach Simon called out.

"Hannah's house," another player shouted.

Coach Simon scribbled madly on the board. Then she held it up for all of us to see.

"There," she screamed. "Can we think about this game now?"

She waited for an answer, but no one said a word.

"Can we think about our game now?" she repeated loudly.

"YES!" we all screamed.

Even if some of us did forget about the party and concentrate on the game, it didn't show in our play. We couldn't get the ball past midfield on offense.

"We are not just working on our defense today, ladies," Coach Simon shouted during a time-out. "Can somebody get our offense moving?"

As I sipped on my water bottle, I looked around to find my mother. I spotted my dad and looked around him. But she wasn't there. Then out of the corner of my eye, I noticed a woman standing alone. I glanced over and saw that it was my mother. She used to always stand or sit with my father. *Why aren't they together?* I felt the tears in my eyes. *When is this going to end? Why can't things be the way they used to be?*

"Let's go, Russomano," Coach Simon called out.

I ran onto the field and moped through the first few plays just like my teammates. All I could think about were my parents.

"HUSTLE!" Coach Simon screamed.

I felt bad for being as lazy as everyone else, so I sprinted across the field. For the entire second half I went through spurts of great effort and then returned to half-speed. I heard my mother and father cheering for me a few times, but I blocked their words out of my mind. They had no idea of how much they were hurting me.

We lost 6-1. After the final whistle blew, Coach Simon huddled us together. I waited for her to scream and yell. But she didn't. In the softest tone she simply said, "On the line."

Eyes rolled and players grunted. We trudged over to the sideline and ran our sprints in front of all the parents and fans. Coach Simon pulled her stopwatch out of her back pocket and started timing everyone.

"Nobody can go home until we all beat the clock," she said. "Let's go!"

I couldn't even pick my head up from looking down at the ground. I was exhausted and angry at everyone.

After our punishment, I passed my mother and father without looking at them. I thought about dignity and respect, but kept my head down in shame. My feet burned as I walked into the locker room all by myself.

Chapter Four

As I moped out of the locker room, I stared at the ground.

"Russomano," I heard a familiar voice call out.

I looked up into the intense eyes of Coach Simon, and waited for her to yell at me.

"Good effort today," she said. "Keep your head up."

I nodded nervously as Coach Simon marched past me. I thought about all the sprints, the screaming, and head games. I could still feel my frustration and anger, and I didn't like to feel that way. So I dug deep and found a way to forgive our coach for the ridiculous things she did. I still thought she was crazy. I wondered how God felt about what Coach Simon did to us. I imagined our coach at the gates of heaven and seeing God with a stopwatch. He looked down at our coach and said, "You can't come in until you beat the clock!" Coach Simon started running and gasping for air. God let her go for a while and then let her in. I laughed and hoped that God enjoyed my sense of humor as much as I did.

I walked out to the parking lot and jogged over to my mother's car and opened the door.

"Hi," she said. "Sorry about the game. You'll do better next time."

"We only have a week left and the season's over," I said.

"Just keep doing your best," she said. "I think you're doing just fine."

I sighed and rolled my eyes. I knew she was just trying to make me feel better, but I was tired of losing. "Thanks," I muttered.

"What time is your meet tomorrow?" she asked to change the subject.

"One o'clock," I said. "It's in Johnsville."

"I'm planning on being there if I get all my errands done," she added.

I wanted to ask where my father was, but I didn't. I just stared out the window and wondered if she would ever bring up what was really on both of our minds. I didn't know what to think anymore. All I knew was that when my parents got married, they both agreed that religion would always be a big part of their lives. But when my father began his plans to start a new church, things changed. We stopped praying as a family, except when my father was around. Then my mother stopped teaching Gabe's Sunday school class.

"Do you know this boy who is taking Faith to the dance tonight?" my mother asked.

I shook my head. "Not really," I said. "His name is Anthony. He's on the basketball team."

"I bet your father knows all about him," she added.

Even if this guy was a prince, it wouldn't have mattered to my father. I started to feel bad for Anthony and I didn't even know him.

"Angel if you really liked a boy, I'd let you date him," my mother said. "And do you know why I would let you?"

I shrugged, not really excited about where this conversation was going.

"Because I trust you," she said. "But your father already set the rules. I can never make any decisions. He won't let me."

"Why don't you talk to him and tell him that?" I asked.

"He won't listen to me," she shot back.

"Maybe you should try again," I said. "Try a different way of talking to him."

"Like what?" she asked.

I rolled my eyes. I could not believe that I was using my 13 years of experience on earth to give advice to one of my parents.

"I don't know," I said. "You've known him longer than I have."

We pulled into the driveway, and I jumped out of the car. When my feet hit the ground, I almost screamed. I winced as the pain singed my arches.

"Are you OK?" my mother asked.

I nodded my head.

"I told your father to take you to a doctor," she said.

My mother stormed into the house ahead of me. As I limped through the doorway, I heard her calling out my father's name. He hustled around the corner and asked, "What's the matter?"

"She needs to see a doctor about her feet," my mother told him.

"No I don't," I said. "I'm fine."

"You are not," my mother added. "I'll take her this week."

"I can do it," my father said.

"I'll do it," my mother insisted.

I cringed as they argued back and forth. *It was my fault. If I wasn't such a wimp, none of this would be happening.*

"I don't know why you're arguing," I pleaded. "I'm not going."

Neither of them couldn't afford to take any time off and going to the doctor would cost too much money. "I'm fine," I added.

"We'll decide that," my father said.

"They're not your feet," I shot back.

He glared at me from across the room. "Watch your tone, young lady!"

I forced myself to walk without a limp as I headed to my bedroom. I sat down on my bed, undressed and put on my robe to take a shower. I limped over to the bathroom and turned the knob. It was locked. I banged on the door.

"Are you almost done in there?" I called out to my sister.

"No!" Faith shouted.

"Could you please hurry!" I yelled.

"I'm trying to get ready," she said.

I remembered that tonight was the junior dance. When I imagined how nervous Faith was, I went back to our room. I laid down on my bed and started to pick at my fingernail polish as I listened to the radio. When Faith finally opened the door, I sat up on my bed. Tight spiral curls of black hair hung down on the sides of her lightly painted face. Her navy blue dress clung to her firm shoulder muscles and trim stomach.

"You look pretty," I said.

Faith stopped biting her bottom lip and asked, "Do you think I'm wearing too much make-up?"

"No," I said. "But I'm not Dad."

We both knew that Faith would have to pass my father's inspection, and so would her date.

"When is Anthony coming to get you?" I asked.

"In an hour," she said. "I'm never going to be ready in time."

"You look beautiful!" my mother said as she rushed into the room. She called out for my father and he came to the doorway. The room fell silent.

"You look very nice," he said. Then he returned to preparing dinner. After he left, I looked at Faith and shrugged.

While my mother fussed with Faith's hair, I remembered about hanging out with the Ballplayers. I rushed into the bathroom and took a shower. I sat down in the tub and massaged my feet. I couldn't expect to go anywhere if I was limping around. I dried off and went into my room. A few minutes later, I heard footsteps running down the hallway. Gabe's smiling face popped into the doorway. "We have to set the table," he said.

After setting the table, we all sat down and my father said grace. Ten minutes into dinner, the doorbell rang.

"May I be excused?" Faith asked.

"Yes," my father said. He pushed his chair away from the table and walked to the front door as my sister ran off to our bedroom. My father pulled open the front door and in walked Anthony Higgins.

"How are you?" my father said as he extended his hand. Anthony's eyes shifted nervously about the room. My father was not an imposing figure, but that night he made a stocky varsity athlete look small.

My mother jumped up and introduced herself and our entire family. Within a few seconds, Anthony's forehead began to shine with sweat. Faith finally came out of the bathroom. She rushed around the living room trying to find her purse. I went to the closet and picked out her coat.

"Have a good time," my father said as I handed the coat to her. "Be home by eleven."

Faith's mouth dropped open. "Dad, the dance will just be getting over."

"Midnight is fine," my mother said.

"Eleven is what I said," my father said sternly.

I cringed, hoping that poor Faith could just get out of the house without any more embarrassment.

"Eleven-thirty," Faith pleaded.

My father took a deep breath. "Fine," he said. He shook Anthony's hand and gave Faith a kiss on the cheek. My mother did the same. I thought of how much I dreaded the day that I would have to go through what Faith had just survived. I smiled at my sister as she hurried out the door.

After we finished eating, I helped my mother and father clean up the table and then asked the big question. "Can I go down to Molly's?"

"How do your feet feel?" my mother asked.

"They're fine," I said.

"I don't think I want you walking around more than you have to," my father said.

"It's just down the street," my mother added. "Let her go."

"Why do you always have to disagree with me?" my father said.

I rolled my eyes, knowing I had launched them into another dispute. A few more rounds followed, and then it all ended when my father threw his arms in the air and said, "Fine. Just go!"

After my father left the room, I asked Gabe if he wanted to go with me.

He nodded his head. I asked my mother's permission, and she agreed.

"Be back in an hour," she said.

Gabe and I quickly put on our jackets and hustled out the door before either of them could disagree with one another again. As I walked out the door, I wondered if our neighbors could ever hear the arguing. Some rows of brick houses on Broadway Ave. were attached to one another. Others like mine, stood only 10 feet apart on each side. I walked down the sidewalk opening my ears to every sound around me. One car roared past and then another. I wished our neighbors would raise their voices, just so I could see if I could hear them. But no one did.

"Gabe," I said. "Please don't tell anybody about Mom and Dad."

"I won't," he said and he looked away from me.

I didn't want him to get worried, so I smiled and gently patted him on the back. "Everything is going to work out," I said. "It will just take some time."

When we reached the O'Malley's, we walked by the side of the house and into the backyard. I unlatched the gate and pushed it open.

"Hey!" Wil said. "What's up?"

I smiled at my friends, who were kicking a soccer ball around in Molly's small backyard. Gabe ran up the back steps to play with Sammy, Frankie, and Annie.

"We've been waiting for you, Angel!" Penny said.

"Look!" Molly said and she pointed to the corner of her backyard. I looked over and saw a small red house with a tiny door.

"We painted it!" Rosie said proudly.

Gabe and I walked over and peeked in the window.

"Let's go inside!" Wil said.

One by one, my friends and I squeezed through the tiny door.

"My dad said he built it for Frankie and Annie," Molly said. "But I made a deal with them."

"If we painted it and promised to keep it clean, we are allowed to hang out on Friday nights," Wil explained.

Molly grabbed the stool, and the rest of us squeezed together and sat down on the thin layer of carpet.

"Shut the door," Wil said. "It's cold."

"It's not cold," Molly called out.

"We need a heater in here," Penny suggested.

"No we don't," Molly said. "We're hanging out here all winter. So get used to it."

"I'm not hanging out in an igloo," Wil said. "You're crazy, Molly."

I laughed at my friends. I'm sure most other high school kids would think it was stupid to be hanging out in a fort. But I didn't care. Rosie shut the door, and the room turned black. Molly flicked on a flash light.

"What are we going to do for Halloween?" Wil asked.

"I think we should all be dressed up the same," Molly said.

"No," Penny said. "We don't want to look like a bunch of clones. Each costume has to have some personality."

"We can still look a little bit alike," Molly said.

"How about we go as Ballplayers?" I said.

"Yeah!" Rosie said. "I'll be a baseball player."

"Who are you going to be this year?" Wil asked.

"Roberto Clemente," Rosie said proudly.

"Not again," Molly groaned. "Rosie, you've been Roberto Clemente for the last three Halloweens."

"I read a lot of books on him this summer," Rosie added. "Now I really want to be him."

We all laughed at our little, shy friend who also happened to be one of the best baseball players in the city.

"Do we have to go as a player or can we be something else that has to do with sports?" Wil asked.

"Like what?"

"I'm going to be a giant running shoe," she said.

"Yeah right," Penny said. "We all know how much you love to run."

"I'm kidding," Wil said. "I'm going to be a trophy."

"How?" Molly asked.

"I'm going to spray paint myself gold," she added.

"That will look cool," I said.

"What are you gonna be?" Wil asked me.

"I don't know," I said.

"You're the one who runs your dawgs into the ground," Wil said. "You should be the shoe."

"Nah," I said. "It would only remind me of how bad my dawgs hurt."

"Give me some time," Wil said. "And I'll think of something for you."

"What about you, P?" Wil asked Penny.

"I want to be a referee," Penny said.

"Good idea," Wil said. "We'll need somebody to keep us under control on Halloween."

All eyes turned to Molly. "What about you?"

"I don't know," Molly said as she scratched her head.

"You should be a giant knee pad," Rosie said.

"No, you should be a mop," Wil added.

We all laughed, knowing how much Molly loved to throw herself on the floor.

"I'll be a punching bag," Molly said.

"A what?" Penny exclaimed.

"A punching bag," she said. "You know one of those big heavy bags. My cousin has an old one with a hole in it. He can take the stuff out of the inside and I'll wear it."

"Why do you want to be a punching bag?" Wil asked. "Why not be a boxer?"

"She is always a boxer," Penny joked.

"It will be fun," Molly said.

"How can that be fun?" Wil asked. "You'll be asking people to hit you, Molly."

"I'll be well protected," Molly said.

We all laughed at the thought of Molly running around Broadway Ave. as a punching bag. Molly's face turned red and she grinned.

• • • •

Around 11 p.m. that night my eyes started to get heavy. I sat up in my bed and read over some of my work for Sunday school as I waited for my sister to come home from her first date. When I looked at the clock again, it was 11:26 p.m.

I started to get nervous for Faith as I thought about my father still sitting in his chair in the living room. I bent down on my knees, closed my eyes and clasped my hands together. "Dear Lord," I began. "I don't mean to sound impatient, but I was wondering if there was any way you could please bring my sister home in the next three minutes!"

I started to pace around the room. But my feet hurt, so I sat back down. I looked at the clock. Less than one minute remained. My palms began to sweat. A few seconds passed, and then I heard the front door creak open. I looked up at the ceiling and whispered, "Thank you!" A few seconds passed, and Faith finally came into our room.

"How was it?" I asked.

"Good," she said.

"What took so long?" I asked.

"We stopped and grabbed something to eat," Faith said. "It took a lot longer than we thought. I didn't even say good-bye to Anthony. I just ran out of his car and up the steps."

"I'm glad you made it in time," I said.

"So am I," Faith said. "And so was Anthony. He was sweating bullets the entire ride home."

I laughed as I crawled under the covers. I said a few extra prayers that night including a short one for my sister, and a long one for Anthony Higgins. I also told God how thankful I was that my mother and father made it through the night of my sister's first date.

But I had no idea of how drastically things would change for our family the very next day.

Chapter Five

When I woke up the next morning, I was eager to hear the details of the dance. I rolled over and saw Faith's empty bed. Her backpack was gone which meant that she had already left for practice. I slowly arose and gently set my feet on the ground. I stood up and took two steps. I braced myself for the pain, but felt nothing. I moved toward the bathroom with a smile on my face. I couldn't wait to run.

I walked out to the living room and sat down on the couch next to Gabe.

"What are you going to be for Halloween?" he asked me.

"I don't know yet," I said.

"I want to be a scary monster," he said.

"You're afraid of monsters," I said in disbelief. "Why would you want to be one?"

"Just so I know what it feels like not to be scared," he said. "Monsters never get scared do they?"

I stopped and thought about his question. Before I could say anything, my father called out from the kitchen, "Pancakes are ready!"

Gabe jumped off the couch and sprinted to his chair. As I walked into the kitchen, I watched my mother as she finished setting the table. Then I turned to my father. He stood over the grill with a spatula. This was the way Saturday mornings used to be. I smiled as I sat down in my seat.

"What did Faith say about the dance last night?" my mother asked excitedly. "Did she have a good time?"

"I think so," I said.

"She almost missed curfew," my father added.

My mother dropped her fork and stared at him from across the table. My father glared back at her. No one said a word.

"Are you coming to my meet?" I asked to break the silence.

"Yes," my mother said. "I'll be there."

"I'll be there, too," my father added.

I wished they would say "we" instead of "I" all the time.

"Please pass the syrup," my father asked.

I looked around the table for the syrup. It was sitting right next to my mother. She did not move.

"The syrup please!" my father said loudly.

She hesitated and then finally reached for the bottle. She handed it to me and said, "Please pass this to your father."

I rolled my eyes. I couldn't believe how immaturely they were acting. Neither of them spoke a full sentence during the rest of breakfast. I kept talking just to try and break the silence. But my mother and father continued to ignore each other and us.

When Trina's mom beeped the horn later that morning, I yelled good-bye and jogged out the front door. I couldn't wait to get out of the house. I ordinarily would have preferred the peace and quiet over the arguing. But something about that morning just wasn't right.

"How are your feet, Angel?" Trina asked as we drove off to school.

"They feel great today," I said.

"Good," she added. "You've got to stay healthy for regionals. I don't think I'll make it without you."

"Me neither," Colleen said.

I smiled. Colleen and Trina both knew that I needed them as much as they needed me.

Trina's mom pulled the car over and we all jumped out.

"Are your mom and dad going today, Angel?" she yelled to me.

"Yeah," I said with a smile. "Thanks for the ride."

We all climbed into the van, and joined the rest of our teammates.

"Good morning, ladies," Coach Kris said with a smile. "How about some orange juice for the ride?"

I reached out for a carton, and thanked our coach. I sat down on my seat on the bus and thought of how thankful I was to have such a fun team and a great coach. Then I felt a tap on my shoulder. I turned around only to see Becky's straight face and narrow eyes.

"You ready to run today?" she asked.

I nodded.

"We need two out of you three to finish as close as you can to Maura and me," she said. "We'll win a team ribbon if we do. So let's do it."

I nodded again as she pulled her headphones over her ears. I turned back around and looked out the window. Butterflies fluttered in my stomach. Then I recalled exactly what she had said to me.

"Finish as close as you can to Maura and me."

She could have said do your best, but she didn't. If I stayed close to her, that was good enough. I glared out the window and told myself that this would be the day I would beat Becky White.

After almost an hour on the van, we arrived in Johnsville. We dragged our bodies and gym bags off the bus and walked toward the park.

"We're running regionals here, too," Coach Kris announced. "Pay close attention to every incline, bend and stretch on the course."

"I've run it before," Becky said. "It's a tough course."

"There is an embankment at the top of the hill," Coach Kris warned. "Be ready for it."

A chill shot up my spine. My mucsles tightened. After we got off the bus, we jogged a warm-up as a team and then stopped and stretched. I took deep breaths and tried to relax. Some of us went off on our own and took another easy jog. Others just stood wiggling and jumping up and down. I tried that for a little while, but I still couldn't relax. I sat down, rested my back on the ground and held my knees to my chest. I stared into the white clouds above me, closed my eyes in prayer, and took a deep breath. A few seconds passed and the butterflies were gone. I couldn't wait to run.

We all huddled up and Coach Kris said a few words.

"Carry each other through this," she said. "You may think you're alone out there during the rough spots, but you're not. You have each other."

We hollered a team cheer, and then removed our warm-ups. The teams of runners all gathered at the start. Trina, Colleen and I gave each other five and then focused our eyes straight ahead.

"Runners take your mark," the starter said.

My nerves tingled. I clenched my fists.

"Set," the starter added.

My thighs felt weak. I inhaled a short breath.

Bang! I jumped forward with everyone else. I moved steadily with the pack, feeling my painless feet spring off the ground. I held my spot for the first mile and then made my move. I pulled Trina and Colleen along with me. I looked past the runners looking for Becky. I couldn't see her. I heard heavy breathing behind me. I looked out of the corner of my eye and saw Colleen.

"Come on, Coll!" I said. "Stay with us."

"I can't," she said. "Not today. Keep going!"

Trina and I stayed side by side. We followed the trail as it entered the woods. We ran over a foot-bridge and weaved through the curves. On one of the bends, we made a quick move past one runner. Then another. I felt good. Really good. Then my eyes rose up to the mountain that awaited me.

"Oh no!" I gasped.

"Come on, Angel," Trina said. "We're almost done."

I think I could have crawled up that mountain faster than I did by attempting to run. When two runners passed me from behind, I slowly felt my energy escaping me. The harder I pushed myself, the weaker I felt. *Come on, Angel. You can do it.* I finally made it to the top. Then my eyes locked on a five-foot dirt wall that awaited me. Runners ahead of me leaped up and pushed themselves over it. I focused my eyes on the wall and ran full steam ahead.

"Ugh!" I screamed as I pulled myself up.

I stumbled after I cleared it, and then I got back on my feet. I looked into the distance and saw Trina make her move down the stretch. I wanted to catch up, but I couldn't. One by one, runners passed me. I crossed the finish line so mad at myself that I began to cry. After a few seconds, I bent over and pulled the neck of my shirt over my face.

"What happened?" I heard a voice ask.

I didn't have to look who said it. I knew it was Becky. I ignored her and turned to the rest of the runners who were still finishing. Colleen stumbled across the finish line. I jogged over to her.

"I'm sorry," she said. "I'm really sorry. I felt awful."

"That's OK," I said. "I fell apart at the end. I was the one who should have made it. It was my fault."

Trina came up to us and wrapped her arm around Colleen. Together we walked off to the cooldown area. I searched the crowd for my parents. I didn't see them the first time, so I looked again. Trina's mother walked over to us.

"Way to run girls!" she said.

Trina rolled her eyes as she gasped for air.

"Have you seen my parents?" I asked Trina's mother.

"No," she said.

Coach Kris came over and gave us some words of encouragement, but I didn't hear her. My eyes kept searching the crowd for my parents. *Where are they?*

I sat down on the ground with my teammates, and didn't say another word. I stared up into the white clouds again and tried to settle my mind. I couldn't. So I rolled over and pushed myself up.

Shots of pain rushed through my feet.

● ● ● ●

I pushed open the front door and tossed my gym bag down. I walked up the steps and looked up. My father slipped off his glasses and set the Bible down on the end table.

"How did you do?" he asked.

"Awful," I said.

"What happened?" he said.

"I don't know," I said. "I felt good and then I felt terrible. There was this huge hill, and I should have just crawled up it. It would have been faster."

I looked around the room. "Where's Mom?" I asked.

He didn't answer me. He took a deep breath and stared at the ground. My heart pounded in my chest.

"Where is everybody?" I asked loudly.

"Gabe and Faith are in their rooms," he said.

"Why?" I asked.

"We've been having a difficult time," he said.

I looked at him and began to shake my head in disbelief. "What is happening?"

"Your mother has left for a little while," he began.

My heart sank. *No. This can't be happening. Please God, no!*

"It might be better that we spend some time apart until we can work things out," my father added.

My bottom lip began to quiver as anger spread through me. I burst into tears.

58

"No!" I screamed. "You can't do this!"

"It's the best thing for us right now," he said.

"How do you know?" I shot back. "We're a family! We're supposed to love each other. That's what you taught us. To love each other!"

"Sometimes things are not that simple," he began. "It's not that we don't love each other."

I stopped listening. Nothing he said made sense.

"How can you do this to us?" I yelled as I ran out the back door. I gritted my teeth to fight the pain as I barreled down the steps. I slowed down my jog into a fast walk. I turned down the sidewalk and something made me look up at my house. My eyes stopped on my little brother's bedroom window. Gabe's sad face gazed down at me. My heart filled with shame. I walked back up the steps and in the front door. When I stepped inside, I didn't look at my father. I went straight to Gabe's room and sat down on the bed next to him. I looked up and saw Faith standing in the doorway.

"What's going to happen?" he asked.

"I don't know, Gabe," I said. I turned to my sister.

She turned her teary eyes away from me and she went back to our room.

Chapter Six

When I woke up early the next morning, our quiet house felt empty. *I miss her, God. Why does it have to be like this? They're good people. Please help them work it out.* I shut my eyes tight as I thought about going to church without my mother. My mind raced with fear. *What will people think?*

To the people of our church, we were the ideal family: healthy, happy, and faithful. Religion had always been a vital part of our lives. My father, who was the son of a preacher, grew up in a big family on a farm down south. During his senior year of high school, a friend of a friend set my father up on a blind date with a shy, church-going girl from the other side of town who liked to swim. That's how my mother and father met.

My mother admitted that she wasn't as strong a swimmer as Faith was in high school, but she always held her own. My mother told us that there was no such thing as a swimming scholarship. There was just a pool, a coach, some girls, and 5 a.m. practices. The girls had to practice before dawn because all the boys' teams had the other time slots throughout the day. I told her I wouldn't have put up with taking a back seat to the boys.

"People didn't care about sports for girls and women back then," my mother explained.

When my father went to college to study to be a minister, my mother decided to go with him. Even though she could have had a chance to go to a different college and be on the swim team, she decided against that college and went to a smaller college to be closer to my father.

"I didn't realize how much I loved swimming," she said. "It was so important to me, but I listened to those who told me that swimming meant nothing."

I hoped that my father wasn't one of those people, but I wasn't quite sure.

"Things were different back then," my mother told us.

My parents married the summer after their first year in college. Halfway through school, my mother had Faith. When my father graduated, they decided to move north with some of their cousins and join a church in the city. They had me the first week they arrived. My mother returned to school and earned her teaching certificate. Four years later, Gabe came into our world. The summer before my fifth grade year, we moved out of our tiny apartment to our new house on Broadway. My father promised himself and us that once Gabe was in school, he would go after his dream. His dream was to start his own church.

I lay in my bed for over an hour that morning wondering how, why and when things started to go bad. We were a family. We were supposed to be together. Now my mother was alone. I started to cry. *Why? Why is this happening?*

Then I heard a gentle knock on the door. I closed my eyes and pretended that I was sleeping.

"Good morning," my father said as he pushed open the door. "Everybody up."

I didn't move. Neither did Faith.

"Come on, girls," he said. "Get ready for Sunday school."

I rolled over but did not look at him. It was my parents' idea to have Faith and me take turns teaching Gabe's Sunday school class before church every week. It was my turn to teach a lesson this week, and I didn't want to do it. My father left the room and both of us sat up.

"Faith," I said. "Can you teach this week?"

"No," she said. "I haven't prepared anything."

"I'll show you my lesson," I said.

"Why can't you do it?"

"I don't feel well," I said.

"If you don't feel well, than neither do I," she said.

I groaned in frustration. I usually enjoyed staying up late at night preparing lessons for Gabe and all of his friends, but not after what happened the day before. "I'm not doing it," I said.

"Great," she said. "You know Dad will make me do it by myself. Thanks a lot, Angel."

Faith stood up and stomped off to the bathroom. I changed my mind and decided to cooperate, but I didn't tell her. I just stayed in my bed. I usually went out to the kitchen table and showed my father and mother the lesson I had prepared for the week. But that morning I didn't want to put my feet on the ground, and I didn't want to see my father. I closed my eyes and fell back asleep.

"Get up, Angel!" my sister yelled. I opened my eyes and pulled myself out of bed. I limped to the bathroom, changed, and went out to the kitchen. Gabe sat next to my father eating his cereal.

"Good morning," my father said.

"Hi," I muttered as I looked in the cupboards for a bowl.

"Do you have your lesson ready for Sunday school?" he asked.

"Yes," I said.

"Where is it?" he asked.

"In my room," I replied. "It's finished."

"Aren't you going to show it to me?" he asked.

"We don't have enough time," I said.

"Oh," he said with a frown. I looked away and hurried out of the room.

Just before we left for church, I picked up my lesson folder off my desk. I flipped open the folder and looked at the subject I had written on the top of the page:

Faith

Then I shut the folder and tossed it back on my desk.

"Let's go, Angel!" my father yelled.

I didn't move. *I'm going to tell him that I'm not going. He can't make me.* Then I heard footsteps running down the hall. Gabe appeared in the doorway. "Aren't you ready yet?" he asked.

A lump formed in my throat and my shoulders drooped as I looked into my brother's wide eyes. I tucked the folder under my arm and followed Gabe down the hallway.

• • • •

I opened the door of a small room in the back of church.

"Angel! Angel!" a little girl called out as she ran up to me.

"Faith! Faith!" another cheered.

The group of third graders laughed and giggled as they scampered about the room. I couldn't help but smile.

"Let's get them started," Faith said. We walked around the room and slowly talked each child into sitting down in the row of chairs.

"Can't we just play today?" a little boy asked me.

I hesitated and wanted to tell him that I was all for play that day.

"We have so many great things to learn today!" I said with a smile.

The room quieted, and Faith led with the opening prayer. As she spoke, I watched the children. Some smiled as they listened quietly. Others stared at the ground. Gabe pressed his hands together in front of his face and shut his eyes tight. I closed my eyes and listened to my sister's words:

"Trust in God...Love one another...Hold on to your faith."

I then opened my eyes and looked at her, wondering if she had any doubt.

"Angel has planned a lesson for us today," Faith announced. "And if we work hard and finish it, we can play a game for prizes!"

Everyone cheered. I smiled at my brother, and he grinned back at me. With my mind focused on the children, the hour passed quickly. After we dismissed the children, I went out into the hallway with Gabe and Faith. My father greeted us with a smile. He hugged me with one arm and Gabe with the other.

"How was Sunday school today?" he asked.

"Good," Gabe said.

"What did you learn?" my father asked.

"Lots of stuff," my brother said.

My father shook his head and grinned. I turned and watched all the people come in the doors of the church. Mrs. Robinson slid off her coat and greeted us with a warm smile. "How are you all doing this morning?" she asked.

"Just fine, Mrs. Robinson," my father said.

Mrs. Robinson looked around the room. "Where's your wife?"

My nerves tingled and my stomach muscles tightened. My father hesitated and then said, "She couldn't make it today."

I held my breath as Mrs. Robinson's eyes narrowed.

"Is she sick?" Mrs. Robinson asked.

"No," my father said politely. Then he turned and smiled at another family as they walked through the front door. Mrs. Robinson's brow furrowed as she looked at us. I smiled nervously and then followed Faith as she walked away.

Once the service began, I relaxed. My father's voice did not waver once during his sermon, but he kept wiping his brow with a handkerchief more than he usually did. I missed my mother, and I hoped that my father did, too. I wanted so badly for her to be sitting with us. I looked around at all the people in the church who smiled as they listened closely to my father. It would only be a matter of time before they found out. *What would they think? What would they say?*

After church, a few people asked about my mother. All our father kept saying was, "she couldn't make it today." While I was thankful that he did not lie nor did he ask us to lie for him, I still couldn't wait to get out of the building.

On the way home in the car, my father turned off the radio. This meant that he had something important to say and needed our attention. We all stopped talking.

"I want you all to know how proud I was of you today for carrying yourselves the way you did," he said. "I know this is hard on you. It's a difficult time for all of us."

I wanted him to say he was sorry, but he didn't. He turned the radio back on. I watched him stare out the window. My heart pounded in my chest.

"Can I go down to the park today?" Gabe asked.

"I'll take you," I blurted out.

My dad pulled into the driveway and we all jumped out. I felt the pain return. I took a few slow, easy steps.

"I'm concerned about your feet," my father said. "I'm taking you to the doctor this week."

"I'm OK," I assured him. "They just get a little sore."

"I don't like you to limp around like that," he said.

I straightened myself up. "I'm fine," I pleaded.

He raised his eyebrows at me and said, "I don't think so."

When we walked into the house, the phone rang. I walked over and picked it up.

"Hi, honey," my mother said softly.

I hesitated for a second. "Hi," I finally said. "Where are you?"

"I'm at your cousin's," she said. "I'm OK. Don't you worry about me."

"When are you coming back?" I asked.

"I don't know yet," she said. Then her voice cracked. "I'll call you every day. I'm going to be at your game and your cross-country meets. Don't you worry."

I could tell by her voice that her eyes were filled with tears.

"Can I talk to Gabe and Faith?" she asked.

I put my brother on the phone and stood next to him as he listened. He said "Uh-huh," and added, "I love you, too." Then he handed the phone to my sister. She said the same and then hung up.

"Can we go to the park, now?" Gabe said.

"Yeah," I replied. "I'll go get changed."

Five minutes later, we shed our church clothes for sweat pants, jackets and sneakers. My feet felt good in my soft running shoes. We hurried past my father who was cleaning the dishes in the sink.

"Be careful!" he called out as we ran out the back door.

I kicked my soccer ball as Gabe and I jogged down Broadway Ave. together. When we turned on Woodside and headed for the park, I let all my worries go. I breathed the cool fall air and laughed as my little brother tried to steal the ball out from under my feet.

"Hey, Angel!" Wil called out and I looked up.

I smiled at the Ballplayers as Gabe ran off to play on the swings. Wil came running over to me.

"I heard about something that might help your feet," she said excitedly.

"What?" I asked.

"My grandma said that if you cut up potatoes and wrap them to the bottoms of your feet, you'll feel better."

"Are you kidding?" I asked.

"That's crazy!" Penny said.

"I'm asking my mom," Molly said. "She'll know."

"My grandma says it worked for her," Wil said.

I shook my head and grinned. I couldn't imagine slicing up some potatoes and sleeping with them on my feet all night. Then again, Wil was a straight A-student. So smart that she never got a B in her life. I put the potato thought in the back of my mind.

"What are we playing today?" I asked.

"A little bit of everything," Penny said.

"Let's shoot some hoop!" Molly called out.

"We always shoot hoop," Wil said.

Rosie looked up from under the bill of her cap and asked, "How about some baseball?"

"We played that all day yesterday," Molly groaned.

"Let's take a vote," Penny called out.

"Fine," Molly said.

When every one of my friends voted for a different sport, Penny threw her hands up and said, "So much for that!"

As we laughed and joked, I kept kicking my soccer ball around. I tapped the ball over to Penny and she kicked it to Molly.

"Yo!" Wil called out. "Pass it over here!"

Molly tossed her basketball on the grass and kicked a hard pass over to Wil. Rosie snuck in front of her and took the ball away. Wil chased her down and stole it back.

I grinned proudly. What started as a little drill turned into a full game. Slowly the kids from Broadway joined us and we took over the open playing field. We used baseball hats and basketballs as goal markers. I ran around the field and worked as hard as I could, and so did my friends.

I wanted to run and play forever.

Chapter Seven

"WORK, ladies, WORK!" Coach Simon screamed.

I pumped my arms and clenched my fists as we ran through our last series of soccer drills and sprints for the day.

"Two more games and this is over," one player muttered between breaths. "I can't wait."

I glared at her. I knew my teammate didn't care about our season, but she didn't have to say it. As sick and tired as we all were of running and losing, I still wanted to win our last two games.

"What is Coach Simon trying to do?" another player whined. "We have a game tomorrow!"

"You can run faster!" Coach Simon yelled. "Come on, dig deep!"

Coach Simon's shouts only drove us further apart.

"One more lap," she shouted. "Run this one for me!"

We all moaned. Our goalie stumbled and caught herself just before she hit the ground. Another teammate grabbed onto her arm and pulled her through the sprint. By that time, I almost started to complain like everyone else, but I was too tired to speak. I gasped for air as we jogged out to center field for our team cheer. After we huddled up in the middle and forced out another team groan, I started to breathe normally again. I slowly started to regain feeling in my numb legs. We all collapsed on the grass for our team stretch.

"How did they ever give Coach Simon this job?" one girl said.

"I'm not playing next year if she's still the coach," another added.

Within a few minutes, my teammates stopped bad-mouthing Coach Simon and started talking about issues that were more important to them than soccer.

"Hey Angel," a player asked as our team walked off the field. "How come you didn't come to the party Friday night?"

"I had other plans," I said.

"You missed a good time," she said. "The whole class was there. I mean, everybody."

"That kid Jason was there," another girl said. "He kept asking where you were whenever I saw him."

I stared at the grass as I felt everyone's eyes on me. They were waiting for me to say something about Jason Mitchell, who was the captain of the freshman soccer team. I talked to him before math class almost every day.

"Do you like him?" our goalie blurted out.

"He's nice," I said. "But I don't really know him that well."

Just as the last word came out of my mouth, the entire boys' soccer team jogged up over the hill. All the girls laughed and giggled. Some waved as the boys passed. I looked up curiously and saw Jason leading the pack. Jason turned in our direction and I glanced away. I liked boys, but they made me nervous for one big reason. My father's rule was that Faith and I could not date until our junior year. The problem was that I kind of wanted to go out with boys. Just to the movies or out to play sports. I didn't think there was anything wrong with that. I asked my father once if it would be OK. Although I didn't have any boy in mind at the time, I was just curious to see what I could negotiate with my father.

"May I just shoot baskets down at the park or play tennis with a boy?" I asked.

"As long as you're with your friends or a group of kids," he said.

"What about the movies?" I asked.

"You may go only with your girlfriends," he said.

"Come on, Dad," I said. "What's the big deal if a few boys come with us? We're all just friends."

"Angel," he said firmly. "You know the rules."

After the boys passed, my teammates turned to me again.

"Is it true that you aren't allowed to date?" one asked.

I didn't answer. They didn't understand how disappointed and upset my father would have been with me if I broke one of his strictest rules.

"That's what I heard about your sister," the girl said. "You two can't date until you're 16."

I pulled a brush out of my bag and nervously started stroking my hair. It bugged me that they knew private things about my family. They had no business judging me. I frowned as I quickly tied my hair up in a pony tail and stood up.

"I'm not trying to be mean," she said. "I was just curious."

I looked at this girl, amazed that she did not realize how nosy she was being.

"Does your father let you go to the parties?" another girl asked. "Is that why you don't hang out with us?"

"No," I said. "I like to hang out with some of my friends in my neighborhood, that's all."

"You don't drink do you?" one asked.

I shook my head as I kicked off my cleats.

"Smoke?" another blurted out.

"No," I said. "Do you?"

"No," she said. "But I tried it once."

I didn't understand what the point was of trying something when I knew that I'd never want to do it.

"You don't curse or swear?"

I shook my head.

"Do you like any boys?" another asked.

"Yes," I said. "Do you?"

"Yeah," she shot back defensively. "I've got a boyfriend."

I shook my head again and laughed. I guessed the only way I could prove that I liked boys was if I had one to claim as my own.

"What are you laughing at?" she asked.

"Nothin'," I said.

"Isn't your father a preacher?" a girl asked.

"Yes," I said.

"Is that cool with you?" she said.

I nodded. "Yeah," I said. "Why wouldn't it be?"

She shrugged. "I don't know," she said. "I was just wondering." I decided it would be best just to walk away from this conversation. I quickly changed into my running shoes, said good-bye to my teammates, and hustled over for cross country practice.

As I jogged off, I promised myself that the next time I was around people who talked about me, I'd ask them all just to call me, "Angel the Dork." This way they would feel more comfortable just saying how boring they thought I was. I grinned at my thoughts. Each step grew lighter as I slowly began to leave all of my worries behind.

"Hey there!" Coach Kris said with a smile. "Slow down!"

I jogged up to my coach and then stopped. I looked around frantically for my teammates. "Sorry I'm late," I said.

"You're not late," Coach Kris assured me. "We just started a little early today."

"What should I run?" I asked.

"I want you to sit out the warm-up and just focus on the last sprint," she told me.

I looked up in surprise at my coach, but didn't say anything.

"I know how hard you've been working at soccer practice," she began. "And I want to be careful not to burn out your legs before regionals."

"I'm fine," I said. "I'm not tired. I never really get tired."

"I know how tough you are, Angel," she said. "But I'm worried about those feet of yours, too. How do they feel?"

"Fine," I said.

"I'm going to talk to your parents this week just to keep an eye on you," Coach Kris warned.

A chill shot up my spine. I didn't want Coach Kris within 10 feet of my parents. The thought of my coach's finding out about my troubles at home made me sweat. "My feet are all right," I said. "Don't worry."

74

"I don't want you trying to do too much," Coach Kris said. "I think you really have a shot at qualifying for regionals."

My eyes grew wide and butterflies fluttered in my stomach.

"I want you to catch Becky today in the interval runs," Coach Kris said. "If your legs are fresh, I really think you can stay on her tail."

I nodded my head and felt a rush of adrenaline. I couldn't wait to run.

"Stretch out," Coach Kris said. "I'm going up around the bend to bring them in. We'll start the interval in a few minutes."

I nodded my head again and started my series of stretches as my coach jogged off. I jiggled my legs one at a time. I then rotated my shoulders in their sockets and bent down to touch my toes. My body felt warm and my muscles felt loose. I couldn't wait to run.

I looked up in the distance and saw Becky kicking the last stretch of the run. Maura ran about 50 yards behind, and then Trina and Colleen followed. As she grew closer, Becky slowed down to a jog. Then she walked over to me.

"Where've you been?" she asked.

I didn't know what to say. I didn't want to sound like Coach Kris was treating me better than anyone else. Then I thought of saying something really cocky like, "I'm waiting to beat you." But that's something Becky would say.

"I was late," I replied.

One by one, the rest of the team finished their runs. Some grabbed a quick sip of water and others stretched out. Within a few minutes, Coach Kris called us all together.

"It's interval time," she said. "I want a hard jog to the entrance of the football field, and then a 100-yard sprint to the far goal post. Then I want a steady, easy jog over the hill. Once you hit the baseball dugout, I want a full sprint back to me. I'm putting you in groups of three."

I looked around at my teammates, who did not seem nearly as excited as I was.

"Becky, Maura and Angel," Coach Kris said. "You're up first."

I turned to Trina and Colleen and they grinned. "You can do it," Trina whispered.

I stood in between the two best runners on our team and waited. And waited.

"Ready...,"Coach Kris said. "Set...go!"

What was supposed to be a hard jog was a full sprint for me. I stayed right with them all the way up to the football field. Then I began to wonder how I was going to pick up my speed. I already felt as if I were in a full sprint. *Pick it up, Angel. Pick it up! You can do it!* Becky pulled ahead and Maura did the same. I pumped my fists and gritted my teeth. *You've got to breathe, Angel! Don't forget to breathe!* I sucked in steady breaths of air and closed the gap. We turned down the hill together for our easy jog. The momentum from the hill almost sent me crashing to the ground. I focused on my every step. Slowly I regained my stride.

"Bring it in!" Coach Kris cheered. "Come on, bring it in!"

Becky started to grunt and groan.

"Try and stay with me," she muttered.

Right then she turned on the burners. I looked at her heels and wondered if she had tiny propellers attached to her sneakers. But as I watched her heels, I stayed on them, and so did Maura. *Keep it steady, Angel. Hang on! Don't lose her now! Hang on!*

Maura and I hung on for another 50 yards and then Becky slipped out of our reach. There was no catching her. Maura and I sprinted down the last stretch and crossed the finish line. Coach Kris clicked her stop watch and said, "Nice job! Way to push each other. Way to work!"

We all cheered in between gasping for breath as the rest of the runners finished.

"Way to run, Angel," Trina said.

"How'd you do it?" Colleen asked.

I shrugged and did not smile. I looked past my friends and my eyes stopped on Becky.

"You're going to catch her," Trina whispered. "I just know it."

"One mile cool down," Coach Kris announced. "Nice and easy."

Our team moved together and slowly began our run.

"Angel," Coach Kris called out, "come here."

I turned around and jogged back.

"Excellent job today," she said. "I want you to remember how you made it up that hill. Steady and easy. You didn't beat yourself up trying to get up it. You took every step one at a time. I was far away, but I could see how focused you were."

"Thanks," I said.

"Don't be down on yourself," she said. "You should be proud!"

I exhaled and shook my head.

"Think of how much you've already improved!" Coach Kris added.

I thought of the first day of practice and how much I wanted to be able to keep up with Maura. I

77

smiled knowing that I was that much closer to Becky.

"I want you to go home and get some rest," she said. "Soak those feet and get them up. Regionals will be here before you know it."

I looked in the distance and started to feel bad for leaving so soon.

"Go ahead," Coach Kris said. "Don't worry about it."

Becky turned over her shoulder and glared at me.

• • • •

I walked in the back door and Faith followed me in.

"Hi, girls," my dad said with a smile. "How was your day?"

"Great!" I said with a grin.

"Tell me about it," he asked.

"Coach Kris had me run intervals with Becky and Maura," I said. "I stayed with Maura the whole way!"

"All right!" my dad said and he smiled. "I want you to call your mother and tell her about it. She's very proud of the way you've been working. We both are."

It felt good hearing him say nice things about my mother. I picked up the phone and called her. She answered and I told her all about it. She promised me she'd be at the soccer game the next day. "Keep doing your best, honey. We're so proud of you!"

I smiled and she said good-bye. I was so glad to hear happiness in her voice and see it on my dad's face. After dinner, he gave me an extra piece of pie for dessert.

"That's for holding your own today," he said. "You deserve it."

"What about us?" Faith said with a smile.

"You can scrape what's left out of the dish," he joked.

I smiled and laughed with Gabe and Faith at the table. Then I cut my piece of pie into three pieces and shared it with them. Things were still awkward without Mom around, but I tried to keep thinking of my bright moment that day. I stood up to bring my dishes to the sink and froze in pain.

"Ow!" I said aloud.

"What's wrong, Angel?" Gabe asked.

"Nothin'," I said nervously. I slid back down in my chair, which took the pressure off of my sore feet.

"It's your feet, isn't it?" my dad asked. "That's it. I'm taking you to the doctor."

"No," I said. "Coach Kris said she was going to call and talk to you about my feet first. Wait until you talk to her."

"Fine," my father said. "Maybe she can recommend a doctor."

I cautiously moved about the kitchen in slow, calculated steps. I went off to my bedroom and started doing some homework. But I couldn't concentrate. *Why won't this pain go away?* I turned to my sister.

"What would you do?" I asked.

"About what?" she said.

"If your feet hurt like mine, would you go to the doctor?"

"Yeah," she said.

"But what if you hurt yourself right before states?" I asked. "Would you still go?"

"Yes," she said.

"Oh, come on," I said. "You're lying."

"I know it's not that easy," she said softly. "But don't hurt yourself, Angel. You have all of us worried."

"Soccer ends this week," I said. "Maybe it won't hurt as much next week."

"Just be careful," Faith said.

When Faith and I started getting ready for bed, the pain continued to throb in my feet. I decided that I couldn't take it anymore. When Faith stepped into the bathroom, I snuck into the kitchen. I looked in the cupboard under the sink and found a sack of potatoes. I took out three and stuffed them in the deep pockets of my robe.

"What are you doing?" Gabe asked.

I jumped and then whirled around. Gabe stood clinging to his teddy bear in the dark.

"Nothin'," I said.

"Then what are those potatoes for?" he asked.

"I need them for a school project," I said.

"You do?" he said.

"Yeah," I said.

"That's weird," he added.

"You'd better get to bed before Dad catches you up," I said.

I walked him into his room, tucked him in and gave him a kiss on the forehead. I then snuck back into the kitchen and grabbed a knife and some adhesive tape. With the light out in our room, I knew Faith was done in the bathroom. I turned on the bathroom light and shut the door. I put down the toilet seat cover and sat on it. I cut each potato and stacked the slices into a neat pile. I wrapped up the scraps and stuffed them in a plastic bag. Then I taped the smelly potatoes to the bottoms of my feet, just like Wil had told me. I grabbed a pair of dirty socks from the laundry room and slid them over my padded feet. I quietly opened the bathroom door, flicked off the light and tip-toed into my bedroom. The wet, hard potatoes slid around in my socks.

I lay in my bed that night and said a prayer. I considered asking God for a special hand in healing my feet. But when I thought of all the sick and starving people in the world, I prayed for them instead.

Chapter Eight

I woke up the next morning and felt the dry potatoes taped to my feet. I draped my legs over the side of my bed and peeled off my socks. "Ew," I said as I winced. A dark gray layer of dirt and mold had stained the insides of my socks. I peeled off the tape and slowly removed the potatoes and my eyes grew wide. The heels of my feet were covered with the dark slime too. I wrapped up the mess and tossed the potato pieces and socks into the garbage can by my bed. I gently set my feet on the ground, closed my eyes and wished all the pain away. I pushed myself up and stood still for a few seconds. My feet felt tight and a little sore, but not too bad. I took one step, then another. The pain didn't stab me like it had all the mornings before. I looked up at the ceiling and thanked God for potatoes.

For two days, I put up with the slime and stuck to the potato treatment. I wanted to tell some of my friends about the magic of potatoes, but I thought they'd think I was really strange. And Faith couldn't find out. If she did, she'd go running to my mother and father. Then they'd think I was really nuts and probably take me to a doctor to check out my head instead of my feet.

Life without pain came to an end much sooner than I expected. During our soccer game on Tuesday, the aching began all over again. When we won, I was so happy about our game, that I stopped thinking about my feet even though they still hurt. Then on Wednesday afternoon, I stood up in the locker room and felt the heavy, inescapable pain creep its way back into my feet. I walked a few steps until the pain had cleared. Then I hustled out of the locker room and warmed up for the last game of the soccer season.

"Russomano!" Coach Simon screamed. I looked to the sideline and watched as my coach waved me over. She stood with her arms crossed and her hands tucked under her armpits. After I sprinted over and stopped in front of her, she looked down at me and said, "I just want you to know that I've been proud of the way you've played this season. In practice and in the games. You're a great player to coach."

I stood there for a second in disbelief. "Thanks," I muttered.

"Hustle back out there and warm-up!" Coach Simon ordered. "We've got a game to win!"

My heart skipped a beat as I sprinted back out to my spot in warm-ups. Less than a minute later, the whistle shrieked and both teams retreated to the sideline.

"All right, ladies!" Coach Simon cheered. "Let's get this one!"

We all cheered louder than we had in the last few weeks of the season. Half the team was cheering about playing, the other half was cheering about the game being the last of the season. I glanced over to the sidelines as I stood on the field.

I spotted my mother. She waved and smiled. My heart ached. I then looked over to my father, who always stood behind our bench. He winked. I wanted to cry.

The whistle shrieked and the movement on the field began. I sprinted to every ball, and kept my spacing on the field. I went one-on-one with a girl from the other team a few times. She was good. Really good.

"WORK, Russomano, WORK!" Coach Simon screamed.

I ran and kicked. I pumped my arms and used my elbows. Nothing worked. I couldn't get past the defense. By half-time, the girl who was marking me had made me look like I was in second grade. We fell behind 3-0. I hung my head as Coach Simon spoke in our huddle.

"Russomano," she called out. I looked up nervously.

"What are you doing out there?"

Then I dropped my head down and stared at the grass.

"I tell you what a great player you are to coach, and you don't do anything I've taught you!"

I felt my face turn red.

"You look terrible out there!" Coach Simon yelled. "Do you even know what you're doing?"

I hung my head in shame. All the confidence she had built up in me came tumbling down. I spent the rest of the game thinking about what my coach said about me. I couldn't move the ball past my defender, and neither could anyone else on offense. We lost 4-0.

Coach Simon said a few choice words after the game, but I didn't bother to listen. I didn't want to feel any lower. I counted on my fingers how many days were left until cross country regionals. Ten days. I couldn't wait to run.

As I walked off the field, I stopped to see my mother. She gave me a hug. I smiled and then looked up. My father patted me on the back.

"Good game," he said. "You tried your best."

I shrugged and felt the tears come to my eyes. Coach Simon had humiliated me, we lost our last game, and my parents didn't sit together. I couldn't stop the tears. I turned my head away from the other players and started walking toward the parking lot before anyone could see me crying. My parents followed.

"Hang in there," my father said. "Don't get too down on yourself."

"Keep picking those points and running to them," my mother said. "Don't stop believing in yourself, Angel."

I wiped the tears from my eyes. I could tell by the sad look in my parents' eyes that I had them both worried.

"I've got to go to practice," I said.

"How are your feet?" my father asked.

"They feel fine," I said.

I waved good-bye and walked off to the locker room by myself. I changed into my running shoes and slipped off my soccer jersey. I threw on a sweatshirt and jogged over to the track.

"Two runs left, Angel," Coach Kris said as I stopped next to her. "Are you stretched out?"

I nodded as I walked over and lined up next to Trina and Colleen.

"Run with Maura and Becky," Coach Kris told me.

My nerves tingled. Then Becky shot a nasty look at me. I glared back at her for the first time all season. I listened to Coach Kris's instructions, picked my points and ran as steady and as hard as I could. I finished tied with Maura after the first race, and then fell apart at the end of the second. As I crossed the finish line, I wanted to cry all over again.

"You beat yourself up on that hill again," Coach Kris said. "Slow and steady. Take one step at a time."

I nodded my head as I gasped for air. *Stop feeling sorry for yourself! Have some pride!* I felt the tears building inside of me. *Don't cry! Not here! Not in front of everyone!* I turned to my teammates and started to cheer as loud as I could.

"Do you think you're going to make it?" Becky asked me.

"Make what?" I asked.

"Regionals," she said.

I shrugged and then eyed her suspiciously. *What does it matter if you think I have a shot at making regionals?*

"Well, do you?" she asked again.

"Do you think you're going to make it?" I asked.

She scoffed. "Yeah," she said. "I made it the last two years."

Even though I already knew how many years Becky had made regionals, I just felt like asking to get under her skin. At regionals last year, Trina told me that Becky missed qualifying for the state meet by two seconds. I didn't understand why she was so worried about a little freshman like me.

"I think you'll make it," she said.

My mouth dropped open. I couldn't believe that Becky was giving me a compliment.

"Just try to stay with me, and you'll make it," she added.

I shook my head. Just when I thought she was trying to be nice, she fooled me again. I'd never been around a runner who was cockier than Becky White.

"I'll stay with you all right," I said. "Don't you worry about me."

After practice, Trina, Colleen and I went into the locker room. Some of the soccer players were still hanging out.

"What's up?" our goalie said.

"Nothin'," I said.

"Are you coming to the Halloween party this Friday night?" the goalie asked us.

Trina and Colleen both said yes.

"What about you, Angel?"

"I don't know yet," I said.

"Where are you going?" Trina asked me.

"I might hang out with some of the friends from my neighborhood," I said.

"Everybody else is going," the goalie said. "It's going to be a blast!"

"Why don't you stop by?" Colleen asked.

I shrugged. "I don't know," I said.

"Come on, Angel," Trina said. "Just for a little while?"

"Maybe," I said.

• • • •

Later that night, my sister Faith walked into our room and threw her bag down on our floor. I glanced up from my homework. She took her baseball cap off her wet hair and tossed it on her bed. I looked at her pale face and bloodshot eyes.

"What's wrong?" I said.

"Nothin'," she muttered.

"Did you have a meet today?" I asked.

"No," she said. "I had one yesterday."

"You did?" I gasped.

She nodded.

"I'm sorry I missed it, Faith," I said. "I'm so sorry!"

"Don't worry about it," she assured me. "I stunk."

"Well, how was practice today?" I asked.

"I stunk even worse than I did yesterday," she said.

I wanted to tell her to hang in there and that everything would be okay. But I always told Faith that, and she never really seemed to appreciate it too much.

"Coach Simon told me that I was terrible today in front of the whole team," I said. "I think Mom and Dad even heard it."

"Try not to let her get to you," Faith said.

"When is your next meet?" I asked.

"Friday," she said.

"I'll be there," I said.

"You don't have to go," she said. "It's Halloween. Go out with your friends."

"I want to go," I said. "I don't care about Halloween."

"Don't worry about it," Faith insisted. "Mom or Dad will be there even if they still aren't talking to each other."

The room fell silent. I wanted Faith to tell me how she really felt. If she told me, then I would tell her.

"What are you thinking?" I asked.

"About what?" she asked.

"You know," I said. "Mom and Dad."

Her eyes shifted nervously about the room. She looked down at her book bag and started pulling out her books.

"I don't know, Angel," she said. "It's hard going to church and seeing Dad up there talking about all the things we all believe in. Then to see it all fall apart right in our own house. We're not supposed to let that happen to us."

I looked up at my sister and felt her pain. Just as the words flew up my throat, the phone rang. Faith jumped to it.

"Hello," she said and then she paused. "Just a minute please."

She handed the phone to me and said, "It's Wil."

I grabbed the receiver and said hello.

"What's up?" Wil said.

"Nothin' much," I replied. "What's going on?"

"I just wanted to call and check if you've thought of a costume yet," she said.

I hesitated. I didn't know what to say about my plans for Friday night.

"I might go to my sister's meet," I said.

"No," Faith insisted. "You go out with your friends."

Then I thought of the possibility of going to the high school party with Trina and Colleen. I didn't know how the Ballplayers would take it.

"I don't know what I'm going to do," I told Wil.

"What are you going to be for Halloween?" she asked.

"I don't know," I said.

"How about you be an equipment manager?" she said. "Then we can just give you a whole bunch of stuff to carry around."

"All right," I said.

"We're meeting at Molly's after school," she said.

"I've got cross country practice," I said.

"We know," Wil said. "What time are you finished?"

"I'll be home by five," I said.

"We'll come and get you then," she assured me. "I can't wait."

I started to think about the Ballplayers' going out of their way to get me when I still wasn't sure if I was going with them.

"Wil," I began. "I don't know if..."

I paused and then took a deep breath.

"What?" she asked.

"Make it five-thirty," I said. "I'm going to get something to eat."

"Are you sure?" she asked.

"Yeah," I muttered.

"Are you sure you're sure?" Wil asked.

I huffed in frustration.

"Angel," Wil said seriously. "I called you about something else, too. You don't have to answer this if you don't want to."

Wil hesitated.

"What?" I said.

"Is everything OK at home?" she asked.

"Yeah," I said nervously. "Why?"

"You haven't been acting right."

A chill shot up my spine. By the tone of Wil's voice, I had a feeling that somebody on Broadway had heard about my parents. "I'm fine," I said.

"I know I'm not a person who should go around preaching about how important it is to talk about some things," she said. "But we're all here if you need us."

With all of the difficult things Wil had been through, I thought about how much it must have taken for Wil to say that to me.

"Thanks," I said softly.

"See ya Friday," she added.

We both hung up. I felt the tears build up inside of me. My closest friends knew about my parents. The whole neighborhood was probably talking about us.

"What are we gonna do?" I asked Faith.

"About what?" she asked.

"Mom and Dad," I said.

"All I do is pray," she said.

"So do I," I said.

"I want to do more," Faith added. "But I don't know what else we can do?"

"Do you believe that things are going to work out?" I asked.

"Yeah, I guess so," Faith said.

"What do we do when the neighborhood and people at church find out?" I asked. "What do we say?"

"Nothing," she said. "They have no right to judge."

"They will though," I said. It was only a matter of time before the whole neighborhood and congregation found out about our family. My friends were already worried about me. I didn't want to have to tell them face-to-face. I flipped open a notebook and tore out a blank sheet of paper.

Dear Wil,

Hi! There's a reason I might be acting a little weird lately. I'm sorry that I haven't told you or the rest of the Ballplayers this sooner. My mom and dad haven't been getting along. Last week my mom left our house. I don't know what's going on. It's all hard to explain so I was hoping that you could tell the Ballplayers. But please, <u>please</u> tell them not to ask me about my parents. I think I might understand a little bit about why it's so hard for you to talk about your mom. I love them both so much and it hurts me to see them so unhappy.

I'm a little scared. But I pray a lot and that makes me feel better. I will say another prayer for you and your mom tonight. Thank you for being such a <u>great</u> friend!

Love,
Angel

P.S. I can't wait for Halloween!

Chapter Nine

With my father at a meeting on Thursday night, my mother came home and made us dinner. After I set the table, I sat back down in the living room and finished my homework. My mother opened the cupboard under the kitchen sink and called out, "Where are all the potatoes?"

I kept my eyes on my homework.

"Angel," she said, "where are the potatoes?"

"I don't know," I said nervously. Instead of sneaking out to the kitchen every night, I kept the sack of potatoes under my bed. "They must be gone," I added.

"Your father doesn't like potatoes," she said. "He never bakes them."

"I think he did," I said. "Will you help me with this question?"

When my mother walked over and looked down at my textbook, she forgot all about the missing potatoes.

Later that night, I pulled out the bag and peeked inside. Only four were left. Faith barged into our room. I flinched and stuffed the sack under my bed. "Have you seen any of my socks?" Faith asked.

I didn't say a word. I had already lied to my mother. I couldn't do it again.

"I had to borrow a pair," I said.

"Where are they?" she asked.

"Somewhere around here," I said.

The truth was that I did have two pairs of her athletic socks. Both pairs ended up stained with rotten potato slime. When they really started to smell, I crept down to our basement, rinsed out the socks and hung them up in the back closet. No one would find them there.

"It seems like they're disappearing," Faith said. "I can't even find my nice ones for school."

I had started borrowing Faith's socks to wear to school, too. Before I could answer, her eyes narrowed as she looked at my feet. "What's in there?" she asked.

I glanced down and saw my sack peeking out from under my bed. I felt my face get hot.

"Nothin'," I said. "How was swim practice today?"

"Fine," she said and she sighed deeply. "But who knows how I'll do in my meet tomorrow night."

"I want to come," I said.

"No," Faith said. "Don't worry about it. I have more meets next week. When are regionals for you?"

"One week from tomorrow," I said.

"Wow," she said. "That soon?"

"Yeah," I said.

I waited for my sister to stop talking and go to sleep. But that night she stayed up late doing homework. I lay in my bed reading my Bible. I started to think about my parents again. Then I wondered if Wil got my note. I tried to imagine what she and the rest of the Ballplayers thought when they heard the news. My eyes began to water. I could feel the disappointment. I could feel the shame.

My mother stuck her head in the doorway.

"It's late girls," she said. "Why don't you get some sleep?"

I looked up at her tired eyes and asked, "Are you going to stay here tonight?"

She took a deep breath. "Your father and I might talk tonight if it's not too late when he comes home," she said. "I'll be back tomorrow to take Gabe out for Halloween."

I wanted to ask her so many questions. I had promised myself to try my best to not sound mad or angry anymore. I said softly, "Are you ever coming back?"

Our mother walked into our room and sat down on my bed. She rubbed her hand on my forehead and stroked my hair.

"We're trying our best to work things out," my mother said. Her voice shook, but she fought back the tears. "I want you girls to promise that you will keep doing what you're doing. Stay busy in school and with your sports. We both love you and want you to do the things you enjoy."

I curled up in a ball and stared blankly at the floor until my mother gave us each a kiss and left the room. Faith stayed up to finish her homework and then settled down in her bed. She fell asleep reading a book. I reached under my bed and grabbed my sack of potatoes. I stood up and crept into the bathroom. I took my knife out from under the bathroom sink and cut up my potatoes. As I walked back into the room, Faith muttered, "Hit the light, Angel."

I looked up to the Serenity Prayer hanging on my wall. I hadn't read it in a long time. I stopped at one phrase and read it twice.

..accept the things I cannot change

I took a deep breath and wondered if I was strong enough to accept certain things like my parents not being together. I told myself I was strong enough, but deep inside I wanted so badly for them to get back together.

"Come on, Angel!" Faith whispered. "I'm tired."

I flicked the switch and limped through the darkness.

• • • •

"Angel!" my sister said the next morning. "Wake up!"

I rolled over and Faith gasped, "What is that?"

"What?" I said rubbing my eyes.

"Look at your feet!" she said as she pointed. "What's wrong with you?"

I glanced frantically at my feet. One was bare. The tape had fallen off and the crusty potatoes had fallen on the floor.

"Your feet are gray!" she said.

I sighed and rubbed my sleepy eyes. It was time to confess.

"Promise not to tell Mom and Dad," I said.

Her eyes narrowed in confusion. "What are you doing?"

"Wil told me that if I put potatoes on my feet that they'd feel better," I explained.

"You what?" she said in disbelief.

"I know it sounds crazy," I muttered.

"Has it worked?" Faith asked.

"Kind of," I said. "Some days it seems like it does, and others I'm not too sure."

She rolled out of her bed and walked over to me. She bent over and took a good look at my feet. "That's really gross," Faith said.

"I don't care," I said. "Just don't tell Mom and Dad."

"Why don't you just go to a doctor?" Faith asked.

"I want to run in regionals," I said. "I'm afraid a doctor will tell me I can't."

"Be careful," Faith said. "If it gets really bad, you have to promise to tell someone. Promise?"

I nodded even though I was not sure how much worse the pain could get.

• • • •

At cross-country practice that afternoon, Coach Kris had me run with Trina and Colleen. I wanted to run with Becky and Maura, but I did as I was asked.

After practice, Coach Kris walked over to me. "I want you to be rested up for tomorrow."

I nodded my head.

"You'll run hard next week, and then I want you to take it easy until next Saturday."

As Coach Kris finished talking to me, Becky walked up to us.

"Do you still want to have the pasta party next week before the race?" she asked our coach.

"Is it OK with your mom?" Coach Kris asked.

Becky nodded.

"I'll send over the pasta and vegetables next week," our coach added. Then she turned and walked toward her office.

"Are you going out for Halloween tonight?" Becky asked.

"Yeah," I said.

"What party are you going to?"

I hesitated before I answered.

"I don't know yet," I said.

"Who are you hanging out with?" she asked.

"My friends from my street," I said. "What are you doing tonight?"

"I might go out for a little while," she said. "But then I have to go to my dad's house. I want to get to bed early for the meet tomorrow."

Your dad's house? I stared at Becky and she looked away.

"See you tomorrow," she said as she walked to her locker.

After I changed, I went into the bathroom to clean myself up. Trina and Colleen stood at the sink brushing their hair.

"What's Becky's family like?" I asked.

"What do you mean?" Trina said.

"What are her mom and dad like?" I asked.

"I heard they don't live together," Trina said.

"Oh," I said. "I didn't know that."

"They're divorced," Colleen added. "Just like mine."

My eyes grew wide. "I'm sorry," I said. "I didn't mean it that way."

"That's all right," Colleen said. "I'm used to it."

"I'm sorry," I repeated.

All I kept doing was saying I was sorry. I didn't want Colleen to think I thought any less of her or her family. I wanted to tell her why I was so curious, but I was afraid to tell anyone about my parents.

"Are you going with us tonight?" Trina asked.

"I can't," I said. "I promised my friends from Broadway that I would go with them."

"Come on, Angel," Colleen said. "Just for a little while."

"I can't," I said. "They're already thinking of a costume for me."

"What are you going to be?" Colleen asked.

"I don't know," I said. "Maybe just Angel the Dork."

They laughed. "You're not a dork," Trina said. "Just sometimes."

I smiled and said good-bye. I hopped a ride home with one of Faith's friends. After the car stopped, I ran inside our house just as the phone rang.

"Hello?" I said.

"You there?" Wil asked.

"Yeah," I said with a grin. "I think I'm here."

"We're coming over," Wil said. "Get ready."

"What am I going to be?" I asked.

"An equipment manager," she said. "We've got all this stuff for you to wear and carry around."

I laughed and Wil hung up. I hustled into my bedroom and changed into some sweat pants and a sweatshirt. I grabbed a dish of macaroni and cheese out of the refrigerator and heated it up. Just as I finished eating, the door bell rang.

"Come in!" I yelled.

The front door was locked so I jogged over to it.
"Ugh!" I moaned.

My tight, sore feet did not want to cooperate. I slowed down and opened the door. I smiled as my friends walked inside.

"What's up?" Penny said.

Penny wore a striped black and white referee uniform, black pants and a whistle around her neck. She also had a white and black headband to perfectly match her cool outfit.

"Nice headband," I said.

"You know I'm not the same without it," Penny added with a smile.

Wil walked gracefully through the door. Gold glittered in her hair and all over her body. She posed for a perfect jumpshot.

"I am the MVP," she said. "I'm the biggest, best trophy you've ever seen."

I laughed. When Rosie came in next, I just stood there shaking my head. She wore her Roberto Clemente jersey and carried a bat over her shoulder.

"Guess who Rosie is?" Penny joked.

We all smiled at the youngest member of our tight group.

"Three years and counting," Wil said. "Roberto would be proud."

When Molly O'Malley squeezed by our door and walked into my house, I laughed so hard that my sides hurt. Molly's red face peeked out of a hole cut in a large canvas punching bag. Her arms stuck out the sides. She had round boxing gloves tied to each fist and worn, dirty boxing shoes laced up her ankles.

"This is the punching bag who fights back," Wil said.

"Not today," Penny said. "Molly's not getting us into any trouble."

"I never get us into trouble, P," Molly said with a grin.

Wil handed me a gym bag and said, "Suit up,"

I pulled out a baseball helmet, knee pads, huge basketball shoes, a batting glove, chin guards and a football jersey. Penny reached in her pocket and pulled out a headband.

"This is a special one," she said. "Just for you."

Penny looked at me and grinned. An awkward moment of silence passed and then I remembered. They all knew about my parents. I had been laughing so much that I forgot about my note to Wil. I stared at the ground. Wil patted me on the back.

"Can I still wear my bow?" I blurted out.

"No," Molly said. "Equipment managers don't have bows."

"How are you going to wear the headband and the bow?" Wil asked.

"All right," I said. "Fine. I'll leave my bow at home."

"Good," Molly said.

"Let's get this show on the road," Penny called out. "We're outta here."

As we jogged down our steps, Molly said, "We're going to The Sergeant's today."

"To do what?" I said.

"Just to visit," Molly said innocently.

Shawn Plumley, who was also known as The Drill Sergeant, happened to be our favorite target of jokes and fun. But one day when Rosie threw a tennis ball through an open screen, the Sergeant bolted out of his house and chased us through our neighborhood. I could still feel how hard my heart beat in my chest that day when our little joke almost turned into disaster.

"Yeah, right," Wil said. "We're just going to visit."

"What?" Molly said defensively. "Why does everyone always think I'm the troublemaker? I just wanted to see what kind of candy he's giving out."

"We know what you were thinking," Wil said.

"And what was I thinking?" Molly asked.

"I'm not throwing a tennis ball again," Rosie said.

"I'm not asking anyone to do anything," Molly said. "Geez. I thought you were my friends."

Wil wound up and slugged Molly in the side.

"You know we love you," Wil said.

Molly reached up and slugged Wil. Then Penny wound up and smacked Molly. Molly whipped around laughing, with her fists up as we all moved in on her.

"This isn't fair," she yelled.

"You're the one who wanted to be the punching bag!" Wil said.

Molly worked up a sweat trying to keep us off her. As we walked out of my house and started down Broadway Ave., we ran into the boys. J.J., Eddie, Sleepy, Mike and Billy Flanigan turned the corner and walked right up to us. When J.J. took a look at Molly, he roared with laughter.

"Do I get a free punch?" J.J. asked.

"You'd better watch it, J," Penny said. "She's not like most punching bags."

Eddie walked up and Molly glared at him. "Don't even think about it," she said.

He shook his head and walked away. "You are crazy," he muttered.

After the boys passed us, we continued down the street and stopped in front of The Sergeant's House.

"Let's not do this," Penny said.

"Yeah," I said. "Not tonight."

"Just a little something," Molly said.

"Like what?" Wil said.

"No apples," Rosie said.

"Hold up," Penny said. "There's a sign up there."

We all walked three steps closer and saw the sign.

BEWARE OF DOG

"The Sarge doesn't have a dog," Molly said. "He's just trying to get out of giving out candy. Let's go."

Molly walked up the sidewalk.

"Are you sure about this?" I asked.

"Come on, would you?" Molly said.

Penny, Wil, Rosie and I all looked at each other.

"She's right," Penny said. "He doesn't have a dog."

We slowly moved up the sidewalk and stood next to Molly.

"Ring the bell," Penny said.

Wil reached up nervously and pressed the button. We heard no sound. I reached up and banged on the door.

"You say trick-or-treat, Molly," Penny said. "You're the one who got us up here."

The door creaked open and my eyes grew wide. A beady-eyed man looked down at us. It was the Drill Sergeant. I had never stood this close to him. My nerves tingled. He had to know we were the ones who put lawn animals and flower pots on his grass. He had to know we were the ones who loved to torture him.

"Trick or treat," Molly said with an innocent grin.

"I don't have any candy," he said.

"It's Halloween," Molly said.

"I told you I don't have any candy," he said firmly.

Molly scoffed and the Sergeant frowned at her. Then he put his fingers in his mouth and whistled. We heard quick footsteps and a chain jiggling. The Sergeant pushed open the door. A huge brown dog flew down the hallway and headed right for us.

"AHHHHH!!" Wil screamed.

Everyone bolted out of there. I thought Molly was going to run right out of her punching bag. Wil took off faster than I had ever seen in my life. Even quiet Rosie screamed. I didn't even feel the pain in my feet. I just ran as hard and as fast as I could.

As we ran down the street, The Sergeant kept yelling, "Come back, girls! Come back! I just wanted you to meet Max. He won't hurt you. Don't worry! He's a good dog."

"Yeah, right!" Wil screamed.

Guilt made us run away from Shawn Plumley that day. All the times we spent bugging him had come back to haunt us. This was his way of getting even.

We sprinted madly down Broadway Ave. As other kids watched us fly by they called out, "What's the matter? What's going on?"

We didn't stop and talk. We kept running until we reached the fort in Molly's backyard. No one spoke as we crammed into the fort and fell down on the ground.

"That was not cool!" Penny said.

Then I started to laugh. I thought of how funny we must have looked running down Broadway Ave.

"He did it on purpose," I said. "Just to scare us."

We started to laugh it off as we dug through our pillow cases filled with candy.

"What time is it?" I asked.

Molly flashed the light on Wil's wrist.

"Eight-thirty," Wil said.

"I gotta go," I said. "I've got to run tomorrow."

"When is that big race for regionals?" Molly asked.

"Next Saturday," I said.

"We'll be there," Penny added.

I stood up and pushed open the door.

"I'd better get home, too," Wil said. "I'll walk with you."

Wil and I said good-bye and we started walking down Broadway.

"I'm tired," she said.

"Me, too," I added.

"How are your dawgs?" she asked.

"The same as usual," I said.

Wil didn't ask me about my parents, and I was glad. I wondered about what she felt when her mother died, but I still didn't want to talk about it at that moment. I wanted to wait. Deep inside I still held onto the hope that my parents would work things out. I wanted everything to be normal again.

"On three, we're running," Wil said.

I looked at her and nodded. Whenever we walked each other home at night, we would stop halfway between our houses. Then we would turn and face the direction of our houses and run home at the count of three.

"One, two, three!" Wil called out.

We both took off. I ran through the shots of pain in my feet. By the time I reached the front door, my feet felt fine. I stopped and listened for Wil's call.

"Good night, Angel!" I heard her scream.

"Good night, Wil!" I yelled back.

For the first time in a long time, I was glad to go home. When I walked in the front door, a purple and green mask with bloodshot eyeballs jumped out at me. I knew right away it was my brother.

"AHHH!" I screamed, pretending to be terrified.

My brother Gabe ripped off his mask and bent over in laughter. Then he ran over and sat down on the family room floor and started to dig through the sack of candy in front of him.

"Did you have fun being a monster today?" I asked.

"Yeah," he said. "It was fun for a while."

"Did you scare a lot of people?" I asked.

"Nobody except you," he said. "Everybody else knew it was me."

I smiled. My father walked into the room.

"Hi, Dad," I said.

"I was getting worried about you," he said.

"I didn't break curfew," I said.

"I know," he said. "I just get worried on Halloween. Did everything go okay?"

I nodded my head. I didn't consider getting chased by a dog and running for dear life as something to report to my parents.

"Where's Faith?" I asked.

"She's in her room," my father said.

"How did she do?" I asked.

"She was disqualified," he said.

"What?" I gasped.

I ran into the room. Faith had her head buried under her pillow.

"What happened?" I asked.

"I left too soon on the relay," she said. "We lost because of me."

I sat down on my bed and felt so bad.

"It's only one meet," I said. "It's not like it was at state finals."

She didn't say anything. I wondered if my sister's swimming problems were because of my parents' struggles. I looked up at the ceiling and prayed that she would be strong enough to get through this. Then I told God that I was sorry that I wasn't there when she needed me. I looked over at my sister.

"Don't get mad at me when I say this," I said. "But I'm sorry I wasn't there."

I expected Faith to yell at me for always feeling bad about things. "My shoulder is killing me," she said.

I reached under my bed and pulled out my potatoes.

"Maybe you should try some of these," I said.

I looked at her and we both laughed.

Chapter Ten

O ne mile to go. *Come on Angel! Stay with her!* I watched the runner next to me out of the corner of my eye. I remained steady at her side. Then I decided it was time to make my move. I eyed the bend in the path in front of me and picked the point where I would turn on the speed. I rounded the turn perfectly and blew past my opponent. My feet felt good. Really good. I pumped my arms and focused on the next runner in front of me.

Maura's long black pony tail flipped back and forth. I took my eyes off of her and took quiet, swift steps. Within seconds, I had moved in right next to Maura. She turned her head and glanced at me.

"Come on, Maura," I gasped. "Let's bring it in."

I kept my squinting eyes on the ground and felt my legs burn with fatigue. I stared down at the path in front of me. A cramp gripped my side. I winced as I looked up. Becky White led the way.

"Let's catch her," Maura said between breaths.

I took my mind off my cramp as my arms and legs automatically started pumping. I stayed right with Maura. Together we closed in on Becky. I gasped for air. My numb legs began to burn. As we moved closer to Becky, she picked up her pace. The muscles in her arms tightened and she clenched her fists. With about 200 yards left, Maura and I were on Becky's heels. She groaned as we moved alongside of her. I felt a rush of adrenaline. I was sure this was the moment I had been waiting for. Then Becky took off. My tired legs couldn't keep up and neither could Maura's. We crossed the finish line running on empty.

As I slowed down, my whole body screamed with pain. I tried to walk it off, but I couldn't stand up. I bent over and grabbed my side.

"Stand up, Angel!" I heard my mother's voice call out. "Walk it off!"

I tried to straighten myself up, but I buckled over again. I slowly stood up and turned toward the finish line just as Trina and Colleen crossed. Arms flailed and legs stumbled as they tried to slow down. Trina's face cringed in pain. Tears and sweat ran down Colleen's red cheeks. I didn't have the strength to cheer. I dragged myself over and slung my arm around Colleen and tried to hold her up.

"Ugh!" she moaned.

All three of us sucked in air for a few seconds.

"I don't know why I do this to myself," Colleen muttered.

"Well, you're not doing it alone," Trina said as she continued to gasp for air. She turned to me, shook her head and said, "I just about knocked myself out trying to keep up with you back there."

We continued to suck in the cold air. It burned my dry throat.

"What were you trying to do?" Trina gasped as she stared at me. "Give us a heart attack?"

I still couldn't speak.

"Way to go, Angel," Colleen said and she huffed. "You're going to make it next week."

I smiled as I thought about my two favorite running partners. After all the times they pushed me through practice, they deserved to make regionals too.

"Nice job, girls," Coach Kris said. She walked up and patted us on the back. "Way to go!"

I felt another hand on my back. I looked up. It was Becky.

"Way to run, Angel," she muttered.

I thanked Becky. But in the back of my mind, I wondered if she really was sincere.

"Do it next week and you're going to make it," she added.

I waited for Becky to tell me how great she was and how I would never be able to catch her. To my surprise, Becky walked away without saying another word. I walked off to the side to stretch, feeling bad for being so quick to judge Becky.

"Angel!" I heard a voice call out.

I looked up and saw my family behind the fence. My mom looked up, smiled and waved. Gabe started running toward me. I braced myself for his hug. He sprinted over, spread his arms, and ran right into me.

"Take it easy," I said as I patted him on the head. "You're gonna knock me over one of these days."

My mother and father walked over. Faith kept her distance from them and strolled over at her own pace.

"Nice job!" my father said.

"You did great!" my mother added. She wrapped her arm around me. I smiled at the ground. Gabe clung to my side. I tried to unravel his arm from around my waist, but he wouldn't let go. I looked at my sister and she forced a smile. I hoped that maybe my parents were working things out. But when Faith looked away from me, I had a bad feeling that things had not changed.

"Are you ready to go over to church?" my father asked.

I remembered how this Saturday our church arranged for a group of volunteers for garbage clean-up, painting and renovations of certain neighborhoods in the city.

"Is that OK with Coach Kris if we take you with us right now or do we have to pick you up at school?" my father asked.

"Are we all going?" I asked.

"Yes," my mother said. "All of us."

I didn't know what to make of this being a family event. *Is my mother coming because she wanted to help? Or is it because she felt bad for not being around? Was my father worried about what people would think?*

"I'll go ask Coach Kris," I said and I turned away.

As I walked, my feet began to burn with pain. I limped through the clearing crowd and found Coach Kris. I straightened myself up and asked if I could leave.

"That's fine," she said and then she looked me square in the eyes. "Just one question before you go." Coach Kris paused and her eyes narrowed. "How are your feet?" she asked. "I want the truth."

I shrugged and said, "They're all right."

"That's not a good enough answer for me," she said.

My nerves tingled and my legs felt weak.

"Dr. Taylor will be in my office on Monday after school," Coach Kris continued. "She's a friend of mine who's making a special trip just to see you."

I shook my head. "I'm fine," I insisted.

"I have already talked to your parents," she said.

My mouth dropped open. She was serious. I shook my head again. "But I won't be able to run," I pleaded.

"There's no need to worry," Coach Kris said. "Everything will be just fine."

I felt the tears well in my eyes. She didn't understand how much I needed to run.

"Just one more week," I said. "Then I'll see a doctor."

Coach Kris shook her head. "I'm not saying you can't run. I just don't want your feet to get any worse than they already are. You need to take better care of them."

I wondered if my personal potato treatment counted for anything.

"I've been taking care of them," I said.

"What have you been doing?" she asked.

"I've been using this treatment," I said.

"What kind of treatment?" she asked.

I stopped, not daring to explain. If I leaked about my potato secret to anyone, the whole high school would find out. Kids who already thought I was a dork would probably think putting potatoes on my feet had something to do with my religion. I could only begin to imagine the rumors.

"We're going really light this week so you can give it your best for regionals," Coach Kris assured me.

I nodded my head and listened quietly as she spoke. When she was finished, I said good-bye, turned and limped back to my parents.

"What's the matter?" my father asked.

I didn't even look at him. "Why did you make such a big deal about my feet?" I said.

"You wouldn't listen to us," my mother told me.

"Now Coach Kris is all worried," I said.

"She should be," my mother added. "She's your coach, and obviously your feet are really bothering you."

I took a deep breath. I know I shouldn't have raised my voice or questioned my parents but I was mad. So mad about how they couldn't get along. So sick of how much my darn feet hurt.

"Let's get going," my father said.

My brother rode with my father while Faith and I drove with my mother through the city. I stared closely at all the houses on Broadway Ave. and wondered what life was really, truly like inside for each family. I looked into Rosie's bedroom window and wanted to know how much pressure her father put on her. I wanted to know what it felt like to live with an older brother who wanted to play professional baseball and kept trying out but not making it. Then we passed by Molly's house. I was sure that besides the occasional scuffle in the backyard, the O'Malleys had a decent family life. Penny had the coolest Dad and Mom I'd ever met. Everybody in the neighborhood loved Penny and her family. Then I gazed up into the Uptown Apartments and into Wil's fifth floor apartment. We didn't go inside Wil's place too much. There wasn't a lot of room, and her stepmother didn't keep up the place, which I think made Wil a little embarrassed. I stopped thinking about Wil's life. I didn't want to know how it must have been for Wil or for anyone else. I knew what it meant to be in a happy family and I wanted that feeling back.

I turned to my mother and noticed the redness in her cheeks and brightness in her eyes. *How could anyone in a divided family be happy?* As we drove further into the city, I watched her carefully as she talked. She sounded so much more relaxed. She raved about how some of her students were doing in school. She talked about how excited she was to maybe help out with Gabe's basketball team this year. She even talked about how she had started swimming again.

"I get up early before work," she said. "Just like I did back in high school."

My mother parked her car in the church parking lot. Faith and I stepped out of the car, and I limped over to the vans. As much as my feet hurt, I still wanted to be part of the volunteer team. I loved getting together with people from my church and going out into the community. When I looked into the eager faces of all the teenagers and adults, I forgot about the pain in my feet.

With my father behind the steering wheel, we drove off through the tougher parts of the city. I looked around at the run-down buildings and broken windows. I saw a little bit of trash on the ground and a few run-down cars in the parking lot. When the van stopped, I peeked outside the window and saw an older woman looking right at me from across the road. She wore a red beret to match her red sweater. She smiled and I waved.

My father pulled into the parking lot and said, "Let's get started!" We unloaded a bunch of brooms, rakes and garbage bags. Then we teamed up with members of the neighborhood and started cleaning up the sidewalks, parks, and entrance ways of two buildings. Some people passed by with distrustful stares and others did not look our way. I put myself in their shoes and wondered how I would feel if I had outsiders coming in and cleaning up my neighborhood. I wanted to tell them that we did this all the time. Even on Broadway we had leaf-raking parties, car washes, and pick-up-the-park day. I looked up in the sky and took a deep breath.

"What's the matter?" Faith asked.

"Nothin'," I said. "I was just thinking."

"About what?" she asked.

"Do you think some of the people don't like us to come here?" I asked.

"Maybe," she said. "But think of all the people who do like us to be around."

"What about those who don't?" I asked.

"I don't know, Angel," she said. "We're just trying to help. Stop thinkin' so much."

After about an hour, my feet began to ache again. I started to limp around. The older woman in the red beret and matching sweater leaned on a cane as she walked slowly up to me.

"Why don't you sit down for a minute," the woman said. "You look like your feet are sore."

"I'm OK," I said.

"No, honey," she said. "My feet are tired, too. Come over and I'll keep you company."

I set my broom on the ground and followed the woman over to the park bench.

"I'm not as young and as full of energy as I used to be," she said.

I looked at the lines on her pretty face and she smiled at me. Then she slowly reached in her bag and pulled out two bottles of juice.

"Here," she said. "This is for you."

"Thank you," I said.

I sat down on the bench and drank my cold drink.

"What you are doing is a good thing," the woman said. "It shows that you are thankful for all the things you have. A nice house, a good family, and people who care about you."

I thought of the word family and wondered if ours still counted.

"There are too many kids who don't have those precious things," she said. "It really saddens me to think of a little boy or girl who feels alone."

I looked across the park and watched my father sweep the breezeway of the second building. My mother carried a can of paint through the open doors. Gabe and a bunch of little boys I didn't recognize giggled as they raced to catch up with my mother. Faith bent over and picked up some trash. I turned back to the woman. She was gone.

"Let's go inside and paint now," Faith yelled.

I looked around for the woman and still couldn't find her. "Where did that woman in all the red go?" I asked Faith.

"She said good-bye to you and went inside," Faith said. "You didn't hear her?"

I shook my head in disbelief. I looked into the tall building behind me and hoped that I had said good-bye to my friend.

"I told you you're thinkin' too much," Faith said. "Come on. Let's go paint."

Faith and I picked up the brooms and rakes and headed toward the breezeway of the other building.

"Your mother is up on the second floor," my father said as we walked up to him. "I'll be up in a minute."

My sister and I walked up to the second floor and my mother greeted us with a smile. She introduced us to two girls our age, and then handed us some rollers.

"A new family is moving into this apartment this week," she said. "They don't expect it to be all painted and cleaned up. So let's fix it up really nice for them."

Faith and I kept a close eye on Gabe as we cleaned and painted. By late afternoon he had five friends hanging out with him in the second-floor hallway.

"Do you know what I was for Halloween?" he asked his friends.

"What?" a boy replied.

"A monster!" Gabe said proudly.

"Really?" the boy said.

"Yeah," Gabe bragged. "It was so cool."

"I don't like monsters," another boy added. "They're too scary."

"Me neither," Gabe said. "I didn't scare anybody though. Except my sister."

I looked at my little brother and laughed. Then I turned to my mom and watched her paint.

"Are you coming to church with us tomorrow?" I asked.

She stopped and turned to me.

"Do you want me to?" she asked.

I stared out the window. "Only if you want to," I said.

"I'll be there," she said.

• • • •

Later that night during dinner, I thought about my mother's promise. I wondered if going to church together was the right thing to do. I wanted my mother to come with us only if she felt comfortable.

"Are you all right?" my father asked me.

I looked up and nodded.

"You've been kind of quiet tonight, Angel," my mother said.

I shrugged. Faith looked at me from across the table. I thought about what the woman in the red beret said to me about being thankful for my parents.

"Why can't we be together like normal?" I asked. "We all love each other."

No one said anything. Even my father sat at the table without a word. A few seconds passed and my mother cleared her throat.

"I think it would be good for all of us to go and talk to someone who can help us all get through this..." she began. I sat up in my seat and smiled. Then my mother added, "...even if things don't work out between your father and me."

My heart dropped in my chest. I felt the tears rise. I couldn't look at my sister. I kept staring down at my plate and hoped that Gabe wouldn't see my tears. I prayed for strength. I thought about dignity and respect, but I couldn't stop crying. I started to get mad at myself for being so selfish. Then I got mad at my parents for being selfish.

"I can arrange a time with Reverend James during the week," my father offered. "Is that all right with everyone?"

Making me go to the doctor on Monday was already asking too much. I wanted no part in revealing my fears to a friend of the family.

"I've got practice," Faith said.

"Me, too," I added.

"We shouldn't all run away from this," my mother said.

Running was the only thing I wanted to do.

Chapter Eleven

The next morning I awoke with my feet frozen in pain. I didn't understand this injury. *Why does it hurt so badly in the morning when I'm not doing anything?* I rolled over slowly and tried to stretch my legs out. My arches burned. *One more week. Be strong.* I held my breath as I took my first few steps. When I reached the bathroom, I sat down on the edge of the tub and massaged my feet as I let the water run. When I stuck them under the faucet, the heat took all the tenderness and pain away.

"HURRY UP!" Faith yelled.

I turned the faucet off and stepped out. When my warm feet hit the tile, they felt fine. *This isn't that bad. Why am I so worried?*

Later that morning, my mother arrived dressed in a pretty long dress and wearing light make-up. She gave us all a kiss. Even my father.

"I went swimming this morning," she said proudly.

"For how long?" I asked.

"About an hour," she said. "I was going to have you come with me, but I wanted you to rest your feet."

I wished she had come to get me. No matter how much my feet hurt, I would have loved to have gone swimming with her. Just to get out and to do something together would have been nice. Maybe then she would explain everything.

"I'll ask the doctor tomorrow if he wants you swimming," she assured me. "It might be good therapy for those feet."

I rolled my eyes and thought about my dreaded trip to the doctor.

"You're both going to the appointment tomorrow?" I asked.

"Yes," my mother said.

I looked at my father. "It's not a big deal," I said. "Why do you both have to come?"

"We're not even going to start talking about this again," my father said. "It's already been settled."

I muttered in frustration. I wondered how much money it would cost for me to go to the doctor. Then I thought of all the things my father had to do at work and how my mom would have to take time away from her students. I went back to my room and sat down on my bed.

"Come on, Angel!" Gabe said minutes later. "We're going to be late."

The only thing that kept me going that morning was knowing that my mother had kept her promise, which was for all of us to go to church as a family.

At Sunday school that morning, Faith took over and taught the kids a great lesson on saying good things about people. After the lesson, we hung out in the lobby as people entered the building. No one asked any questions about our family situation, except for Mrs. Robinson.

"We missed you last Sunday," Mrs. Robinson said to my mother. "Where have you been?"

"I've been busy with a lot of things," my mother said with a smile. "How are you doing?"

"I'm just fine," Mrs. Robinson replied. Then she moved closer to my mother and rested her hand on my mother's shoulder. In a soft tone, she asked, "Is everything all right?"

My mother nodded and smiled. "Everything is just fine," she added.

There was no doubt in my mind that people had been talking about us. I couldn't imagine what others must have been saying about my parents. I feared somebody would blame my mother. Then somebody else would point the finger at my father.

Later on as I listened to my father's sermon, I wondered if deep inside I truly felt better about the situation. Part of me was pleased to see my mother happy. I was too ashamed to admit that the other part of me wasn't comfortable seeing her so content without us around. On the way out to the car, I looked at my mother and asked, "Don't you miss us?"

She stopped and looked at me. "More than anything," she said and her eyes began to fill with tears. She paused before she continued. "There isn't a second that goes by that I don't think about you."

"Why don't you want to be with us?" I asked.

"That's not it," she said. "It's just a difficult time. Your father is a great father to you kids. I am very thankful to have him watching over you."

"When are you going to come back?" I said.

"I don't know, honey," she said. "I have to find happiness within myself before I can bring happiness back to our family."

Later that afternoon, my mother went back to her cousin's house. I hated to see her go, but I was relieved that our family had all made it through a day without any major arguments.

My father spent most of the afternoon with Gabe on a science project for school. After I finished three hours of homework, I quietly walked past the kitchen table and headed for the back door.

"Where are you going?" Gabe asked.

I hesitated. "Out," I said.

"You're going to the park, aren't you?"

I looked at my dad.

"I don't want you playing ball," he said.

"I won't," I said.

"I want to go," Gabe pleaded.

"We're almost done, Gabe," he said. "Let's finish this."

I slipped out of the door and started walking down Broadway. I heard a voice call my name. I turned around.

"Angel!" Penny hollered. "Wait up!"

Penny jogged toward me. I stood and waited for her to catch up.

"What's up?" I said.

"Nothin'," she replied. "How'd you do yesterday?"

"All right," I said.

"When is the regional qualifier?" Penny asked.

"Next weekend," I replied.

"We'll be there," she said surely.

"HEY!" a voice called out.

Wil came running toward us. I looked into her hair and saw tiny speckles of gold glitter.

"You've still got some of that stuff in your hair," I said.

"I guess I went a little too crazy with the glitter," Wil admitted.

"It looks cool," Penny said with a smile. "Keep it in."

"Yeah, right," Wil said. "I've got to get it out before school tomorrow."

We walked down the street talking and laughing. I wished everything was as much fun and as simple as hanging out with the Ballplayers.

"I've got something for you, Angel," Wil said. "It's just a li'l something before you run in the big race. When is it?"

"I've got a mini-meet tomorrow, and then the regional qualifier is next Saturday," I explained.

"I'll drop it off on Friday night," Wil said.

I felt butterflies flutter in my stomach. I couldn't believe how excited everyone was for me. As we turned the corner, Molly ran up to us and started talking. After a few seconds, she asked about the meet and assured me she'd be there, too.

"But what's with your feet?" Molly said.

"Nothin'," I said and my smile went away.

"My mother ran into your mom," Molly said. "Your mom said that you're going to see the doctor. Are you?"

I didn't answer. I wondered how much my mother told Mrs. O'Malley. It was bad enough that word got back to my friends about my feet. *What did my mother say about not living in our house anymore? Did she tell Mrs. O'Malley about our family problems?*

"Are your feet that bad?" Molly asked.

"My feet are fine," I shot back in frustration. "I don't know what everyone is worried about. My parents are such..."

I didn't finish my sentence. I could tell by my friends' wide eyes that they couldn't believe what I almost did. I almost called my parents something bad. They had never heard me talk like that about anyone.

"You sure you're all right?" Wil asked.

"Yeah," I said as I looked away from my friends.

J.J. ran up to us and asked, "Are you chumps in?"

We all looked at the basketball court and checked out the competition.

"Yeah," Penny said. "We're in."

"No," Molly said. "Not all of us."

Molly turned to me and said, "You're not playing."

"What?" I asked.

I couldn't believe that my friend was telling me I couldn't play. I turned to Wil and Penny.

"You'd better sit this one out," Penny said. "You don't want to hurt yourself this week."

"I'm fine," I pleaded.

"You can't lie to us," Wil said. "We see right through you."

I sighed. It was a stubborn three against one, which meant I had no chance of getting in any pick-up game. Molly and Penny headed toward one end of the court. Wil clapped her hands together and Molly tossed her a ball.

"Let's go shoot," Wil said to me. "I'll sit out with you, Angel."

I followed behind Wil. If my friends hadn't made me sit out, I would have been tempted to break the promise I made to my father about not playing. I walked in silence down to the end of the court. Even though Wil didn't make me talk about my feet or my mom, I had a feeling as we shot around that she was waiting for me to say something. I wanted to, but I didn't. All I could think about was what the doctor would tell me the very next day.

Chapter Twelve

A tall, lanky woman with long black hair tied in a pony tail pushed open the door in the training room. Coach Kris jumped up from her seat and greeted the woman with a hug.

"Thanks for coming," Coach Kris said.

Then Coach Kris turned to me.

"This is Dr. Taylor," she said. "She's one of the best sports podiatrists in the city."

Dr. Taylor reached out her hand and I extended mine to hers. I could tell by the grip of her hand and by her trim, muscular frame that she was an athlete. "Nice to meet you," she said.

I smiled and sat down on the padded table. My mother and father both introduced themselves and shook the doctor's hand.

"Let's take a look at those feet," Dr. Taylor said to me.

As I quickly untied my shoes, my mother sat down in the chair and my father stood over my shoulder. I peeled back my socks. My mother gasped at the sight of the dried potato slime.

"What is that?" my father asked.

Dr. Taylor looked up at me and waited for my explanation.

"My friend told me to sleep with potatoes taped to the bottoms of my feet," I said quietly. "I didn't have time to shower this morning."

A smile spread across the doctor's face. "When you're hurting this much, you'll try just about everything," she said. "I've seen it all before."

As my mother rolled her eyes and my father shook his head in embarrassment, I breathed a sigh of relief. Dr. Taylor was the only one who understood how important it was for me to run. She gently touched the bottoms of my feet. When she pressed firmly into my tender right heel, I almost jumped off the table.

"Does this hurt?" she asked.

After such an embarrassing reaction, I didn't think I had to answer the question. I felt my face turn red as the pain and frustration built inside of me. Dr. Taylor pressed my left foot in the same sore spot. I held my breath. I didn't flinch as bad as I did the first time.

"How does this feel?" she asked.

"It's not too bad," I said.

Dr. Taylor smiled as she shook her head.

"When does it hurt the most?" she asked.

"In the morning," I said. "Or after I'm sitting down and I try to stand up. They only feel good after I'm warmed up. I just want to keep running so the pain won't come back."

"It hurts because after you sit for a while and when you sleep, your muscles get tight and stiff," she said.

After stretching out my tight calves, Dr. Taylor finished her physical examination.

"I want you to hear me through on this before you get too upset," she began. I nodded my head and my palms began to sweat. All I could think about was rushing to the hospital for surgery right at that moment. I felt a lump form in my throat.

"You need time off, Angel," Dr. Taylor said.

"The run for regionals is this Saturday," I explained.

Dr. Taylor had to know how much cross country meant to me. She had to know about my frustrating soccer season. I wanted so badly to make my first year of high school sports a success. I had to have a chance. I couldn't stop now.

"Please," I said. "I've been waiting all season for this race."

"I don't want you to make your feet any worse than they are," she said. "They're pretty bad right now, don't you think?"

I shrugged.

"It's not getting any better is it?" Dr. Taylor asked.

I shrugged again and stared out the window.

"That means your body wants you to slow down," she explained. "You've got to listen to your body. You need your feet for a long time."

I totally agreed. But I still needed to run. One shot just to see if I could make it to regionals.

"I still want to run," I said.

She sighed. "Only if you spend all week in the pool and on the bike," Dr. Taylor said.

A chill shot up my spine as I nodded my head. Then I thought about what she said. I didn't know how swimming and biking would keep me in shape. "I can't run at all this week?" I asked.

"You can run only on Thursday," she continued. "Don't worry about taking a few days off. Trust me—your body won't forget how to run. Promise me that you won't run at all until Thursday?"

I nodded.

"On Thursday," Dr. Taylor added, "You can run two miles and that's it. Is that a deal?"

I nodded again as my heart filled with joy.

"I need to take you to the office right now to fit you for these special shoe inserts that will help you," she explained.

Then Dr. Taylor turned to my parents and asked, "Can we go over to the office to make some molds for orthotics?"

They both nodded.

"The orthotics will be back on Wednesday," she said to me. "You can pick them up in the afternoon and wear them right away to break them in."

She smiled and added, "I hope they work as well as those potatoes you've kept in your socks."

"I hope so too," I said with a smile. I wanted to jump off the table and give Dr. Taylor a huge hug. She had given me the best news I'd heard in weeks.

When Dr. Taylor handed my mother some paperwork to fill out, I sank down in my seat. I thought of how much money it would be for the visit and the special orthotics.

"Do I have to get the orthotics?" I asked.

Dr. Taylor turned to me and said, "Yes. You can't run without them."

I thought about all the pairs of foot inserts I had seen on the racks at the pharmacy. "Can't we just get a pair at the store?" I asked.

"No," Dr. Taylor said. "You need good ones that fit your feet perfectly. You're injured, Angel. You've put yourself through a lot of running this fall."

"Don't worry, honey," my mother said. "We'll take care of it."

I looked down at my feet and tied up my shoes with my jittery hands. Then I wiped my clammy palms on my sweat pants.

I had every reason to worry.

Chapter Thirteen

O n the way home from the doctor's office, my mother and I stopped at the grocery store. While we were in the check-out line, I made a mad dash for the vegetable aisle. I grabbed a sack of potatoes and hustled back into line. I gently set the potatoes on the belt and said, "We're almost out."

My mother shook her head.

"Dr. Taylor didn't tell me to stop using them," I said.

"Do they make your feet feel that much better?" my mother asked.

"Yes," I said. "I haven't gone a night without them."

It was too close to the big race for me to go changing my ways.

"I know it sounds crazy, but I need them," I said. "Please, Mom?"

My mother laughed and said, "Whatever you say, Angel."

• • • •

Early the next morning I felt a tug on my sheets.

"Get up," my sister said. "You're coming to the pool with me."

"I'm what?" I moaned.

"Mom's here," she said. "She's taking you to practice so you can swim."

I groaned and then asked, "Why can't I swim after school?"

"There's not enough room in the pool," Faith said.

My mother drove us through the dark morning. I sat silently in the back seat. Once we arrived at school, I laid down on the bench in the locker room. I couldn't imagine putting my tired body in cold water at such a ridiculous hour.

"Let's go, Angel," my mother said. "This will make your feet feel a lot better."

I slowly took off my clothes and put on my swim suit. I walked out on the deck and my mother was already in the water. The swim team filled the shallow end. I wondered if Faith was embarrassed that her mother and sister were swimming at the other end of the pool.

"Dr. Taylor said you can run in the water," my mother said excitedly. "Just like this."

My mother started running in the deep water as if she were on land. I set my towel on the deck and walked down the pool ladder. I waded over next to my mother and began to run.

"Watch the clock," she said. "Run for one minute as fast as you can, then slow down for thirty seconds, then run fast again. Just like practice."

As I started running, I closed my eyes and pictured myself on the course for regionals. I imagined every bend, curve and stretch. Then I saw the hill.

The mountain. Instead of racing frantically up it as fast as I could, I took a steady, strong pace.

"I'm going to do some laps," my mother said. I opened my eyes and she swam off. I could see how much Faith resembled my mother by the way she moved through the water. I thought of all the years she missed out on competitive swimming. I couldn't imagine how hard that must have been. Then I turned and watched my sister swimming so hard on every lap. She stopped after one stretch and gasped for air. I looked up at the ceiling and pressed my eyes shut. I prayed for strength. Not just for me, but for my mother and sister, too.

● ● ● ●

I almost fell asleep in every class I had that day. I didn't know how my sister handled such a demanding daily workout. I spent most of study hall trying to catch up on my homework that I needed to finish by the afternoon. I couldn't handle falling behind in school right before the big race. I already had enough things to give me stress.

Later during lunch time, Trina and Colleen sat down at our table.

"Hi," Trina said. "Where were you yesterday?"

"I had to see the doctor about my feet," I said. "How'd you do at the meet?"

Trina winced and so did Colleen. "We've had better days," Colleen said.

"What did the doctor say about your feet?" Trina asked.

"The only day I can run this week is Thursday," I explained. "I have to work out in the pool and on the bike instead of running every day."

"Maybe I should try that," Trina said with a smile. "Do you think Coach Kris will let me be your training partner?"

"I don't think so," I replied. Then I looked down at my food. "I feel bad for missing practice."

"Don't worry about it," Colleen said. "It's no big deal."

I stared into the distance and saw Coach Kris walk into the cafeteria. She looked around the room full of high school students. Her eyes stopped at our table. I waved as she hustled over to us.

"Hi, girls," Coach Kris said. "How's everyone doing?"

"Good," Trina replied. "But my feet hurt. Can I go swimming instead of running?"

Trina and Colleen grinned, but I didn't. It just sounded as if Trina thought I was getting off on an easier practice.

"Sure," Coach Kris told her. "What time did you get up to go swimming this morning, Angel?"

"Five-thirty," I said.

Trina's eyes grew wide. "I'll stick to running," she said.

The worst part about my feet was that no one could see the injury, which I'm sure left a few people asking some questions when I wasn't around. I wondered if my teammates really thought that I didn't want to run.

"Angel," Coach Kris said. "Come into the training room for a second. I have something for your feet."

I stood up from the table and followed my coach out of the cafeteria, through the gym and into the training room. Once we walked inside, she sat down on a chair.

"I just wanted to talk to you for a second," she began. "I've been talking to Dr. Taylor."

My heart raced with fear.

"Maybe you shouldn't run this weekend," Coach Kris said.

I shook my head in disbelief.

"You're only a freshman," she said. "You have three more years after this to run."

"I'm fine," I said firmly.

"Dr. Taylor told me that this injury can get so bad that you can't run anymore," Coach Kris said. "Neither Dr. Taylor nor I want to be the one who forces you to stop. So please take care of yourself and let us know if it's too much. Don't be ashamed if you need to slow down and take some time off."

I nodded my head, but slowing down and resting never registered in my mind.

"That was nice of your parents to come yesterday," Coach Kris said changing the subject. "Your mom told me a little bit about what has been going on at home."

Frustration spread through me. I looked away from my coach and wondered why my mother had to do this to us.

"Don't be embarrassed," Coach Kris said. "She only told me because she is worried about you."

"There's nothing to worry about," I said. "I'm fine."

"We just don't want you to push yourself too hard," Coach Kris added.

"I won't," I said quietly.

Then the room fell silent.

"My father left our family when I was 13 years old," my coach said quietly. "I know how hard it can be."

I looked down at the ground. *Nobody is leaving. My mother is coming back. What are you talking about? What did she tell you?* I could feel the tears in my eyes.

"A lot of kids go through this," Coach Kris added. "Kids on the team, too."

After Coach Kris finished, I gladly left the room and returned to lunch. I thought of all the kids who would soon find out about my parents not being together anymore. I wondered if Trina and Colleen knew. I wondered if I should be the one to tell them. On my way through the cafeteria, I looked up and spotted Becky. She walked up to me.

"How are your feet?" she asked.

"They're fine," I said.

"Then how come you're not going to be practicing with us this week?"

"The doctor doesn't want me to," I explained.

"You're not limping," Becky said. "So what's wrong?"

I thought I was going to scream. I gritted my teeth as I stared at Becky. *Do you know what it's like to wake up and be in so much pain that you don't want to walk? Do you know how badly I want to run? Do you have any idea about what is going on in my life?* I took a deep breath and searched for some patience within me. Somehow I found it. I didn't want Becky to know what all this terrible pain felt like. I wouldn't wish for anyone to suffer, even if it was the most arrogant, annoying person on our team.

"Are you sure you're going to be ready for Saturday?" Becky asked.

"Yes," I said.

"How can you run a race after sitting out all week?" Becky asked. "Isn't that going to be hard?"

I looked at our team captain and wondered if she was always this supportive of nervous freshmen with painful injuries. I stared into Becky's doubtful expression and said, "I'll be at practice on Thursday."

As much as I didn't want Becky to feel my pain, I made sure that Thursday's practice was one she would never forget.

Chapter Fourteen

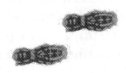

Wednesday afternoon my father picked me up from practice and we went over to Dr. Taylor's office. As we waited in a room by ourselves, I looked at my father and asked, "How much do orthotics cost?"

"I don't want you thinking about the money," he said.

"I'll get a job shoveling snow in the winter," I offered, "or maybe I can start baby-sitting more."

My father shook his head. "You need them," he said. "We'll pay for it."

"But we don't have enough money for things like this," I said.

"Angel," my father said firmly. "Your mother and I can make those decisions."

The door creaked open and Dr. Taylor walked in with her pretty smile.

"Here they are," she said. "Custom-made for Angel Russomano."

I reached out and felt the cork-like cushion.

"They will support your arches," Dr. Taylor explained.

She slid the orthotics into my running shoes. I bent over, pulled my shoes on my feet and laced them up. I stood on the ground and felt a little taller.

"How do they feel?" she asked.

I took one step. It felt like I was walking on a piece of wood. But as I continued to walk, I started to feel sturdy and strong. "They feel great!" I said.

"If they start to bother you, you can take them off for a little while," Dr. Taylor explained. "It might take a little getting used to walking with the new support. But try and keep them on as much as you can."

I nodded eagerly and looked at my dad. He smiled and said, "You look like you feel better already."

"I do," I said as I smiled at my doctor. "Thank you so much!"

I couldn't wait to run.

• • • •

On Thursday morning, I woke up and couldn't escape the pain. I fought back my tears. I wanted to know why my feet hurt me so bad. I thought my three-day rest and my new orthotics would eliminate or at least lessen the pain. But it had come back worse than ever. When I put my feet on the ground, I felt the soreness and tightness shoot through my arches. I took the potatoes off my feet and threw them in the garbage can. I slipped on my running shoes for support and tried to walk into the bathroom. It hurt so bad that I bent down on my knees and started to crawl. I pulled myself up over the wall of the tub and ran the hot water.

I wore my gym shoes with my new orthotics all day long. I limped whenever I could without being caught or questioned by my teammates, friends or teachers. All I could think about during school was how Dr. Taylor said that I was allowed to run two miles in practice that afternoon.

After our last class, Colleen and Trina turned the corner. I stopped walking and stood up straight.

"You're running today, aren't you Angel?" Colleen asked.

I nodded my head nervously.

"How do your feet feel?" Trina asked.

"Good," I said quietly.

"Do you think Coach Kris is going to run you with Maura and Becky today or with us?" Colleen asked.

"I don't know," I said.

As we stretched before our run that afternoon, I thought of the possibility of being at my last practice. If I didn't make regionals on Saturday, the season would be over. I couldn't stand the thought of it.

"Everybody up!" Coach Kris announced. "A half-mile warm-up to start."

I jogged a few steps and then I heard a loud, "ANGEL!" I turned around and walked over to my coach.

"Just take one lap," she said. "You're running one of the intervals with Becky and Maura today. And then a one lap cool down. That's it."

I moaned in frustration and then turned away to catch up with the group. After finishing the first lap, I stopped and let the rest of the runners pass me. I stood on the side and stretched until everyone had finished.

"Are you running with us?" Becky asked, glaring.

I nodded. Becky clicked her tongue and shook her head as we set our places on the track. "How are you going to be able to keep up with us after sitting out all week?" she asked.

I did not answer. I just waited for Coach Kris to say go and I went. For one and a half laps around the track, I stayed on Becky's heels. Whenever she tried to pull ahead, I accelerated right with her. With one hundred meters to go, I stepped to the outside and made my move down the stretch. I picked my point: the finish line. I pumped my arms and pushed my legs until my whole body ached. Then I pushed some more. With about 50 meters left, Becky and I ran shoulder to shoulder. I saved my last ounce of energy for my last four steps. I gritted my teeth and pulled myself over the finish line one step before Becky.

Fatigue and shock froze my mind. Then I realized what I had just done. I had beaten Becky White. As I sucked oxygen into my lungs, Trina and Colleen jumped up and down and hugged one another. When Becky glared at them, they stopped smiling.

"Good try, Becky," Trina said.

I looked up at Coach Kris and she winked. I looked down at my feet and did not know how I ran around the track that day. I shook my head in disbelief as I walked over to Becky.

"Nice job," I said and I reached out my hand.

Becky turned her back and walked away.

Chapter Fifteen

I skipped up the stairs. I couldn't wait to tell my family about beating Becky in practice. But just before I opened the door, my smile disappeared. I stood outside and heard the noise inside.

"You still won't listen to me!"

"Why do I always have to do things your way?"

"I'm trying to do what's best for this family!"

I pushed open the door and walked inside. The room fell silent. I stared at the floor as I moved quickly past my parents.

"How was practice today?" my mother asked.

"Fine," I said.

"How do your feet feel?" my father asked.

"Fine," I mumbled and I turned away. "I have some homework to do."

I shut the door of my bedroom and turned on some music. I spent two hours that night finishing my homework. After a quick dinner, I went to bed at 8 p.m. sharp, knowing how important it was to make sure I got enough rest two nights before the big meet on Saturday. But I tossed and turned for hours that night worrying about everything. *What if they get divorced? What will happen to us? Will we run out of money? Will we have to move?* Then I started to worry about the race. *What if I don't make it? What if I fail?*

The next morning, I woke up and my sister was gone. My mother didn't stop over to pick me up for swimming. I didn't even say good-night to her before I went to bed. I walked slowly out to the kitchen where my father sat drinking his coffee.

"Good morning," he said.

"How come Mom didn't come pick me up?" I asked.

"Your mother and I thought it would be best for you to sleep instead of swim today," he said.

"Oh," I muttered in disbelief. At least they agreed on something.

"Are you both going to be there tomorrow?" I asked.

"Of course," my father said. "We wouldn't miss it for anything."

I just hoped they could make it through the race without arguing. Just once. Just for me.

● ● ● ●

Later at school, Trina and Colleen kept talking about how great it was that I had beaten Becky in practice.

"You should have seen the look on her face," Trina said. "It was total shock."

"I wish I had a camera," Colleen said.

I didn't say anything. While I was glad that I finally beat Becky, the only thing that mattered to me was qualifying for regionals.

"Becky's all nervous about making it now," Trina said. "She's been moping around school all day."

"I bet she doesn't even want to have the pasta party tonight," Colleen said.

"She has to," Trina said. "It's a tradition."

When I saw Becky's scowl at practice later that afternoon, I had a feeling that Becky wasn't too thrilled about being the hostess of the pasta party.

After practice we all jumped in a van and drove over to Becky's house on the East Side. Becky's mother greeted us at the front door. As we walked into her house, I looked around in amazement at all the pictures of runners. At first I thought they were kids of all ages. Then I realized they were all of Becky except for one old photo that wasn't in a frame. A small photo of a lean man running down a path was tucked in the corner of a larger frame. I leaned over to get a closer look.

"That's my father," Becky said to me. "He ran in college."

I leaned back and looked away nervously. I wondered where Becky's father was, but I didn't ask.

"How long have you been running?" I asked.

"Since I was nine," she said.

Then she walked away from me. Obviously Becky still hadn't gotten over losing to me at practice. I kept smiling and talking as if I hadn't even noticed a thing.

During dinner, Coach Kris gave us a pep talk.

"I think everyone is going to do well tomorrow," she said. "I'm proud of all of you."

"How many runners get to go to regionals?" Trina asked.

"The top 20," Coach Kris replied.

I stared down at my plate, thinking of all the great runners in our division.

"The important thing is that you all run the best you can," Coach Kris said. "Don't measure your success by whether you make it or not. Just run and enjoy every second of it."

My mind flashed to the Mountain. I winced at the thought of how much my feet might hurt. *What if I don't make it?* I looked up at Becky. She sat quietly and picked at her food.

• • • •

When I came home that night, I knocked on Gabe's bedroom door.

"Come in," he said.

I looked down at my brother as he played with his trucks on the floor.

"What are you doing all alone in here?" I asked.

"I'm not alone," he said. "I've got my trucks."

I caught a glimpse of his red eyes.

"Are you all right?" I asked.

He shrugged.

"Was Mom here earlier?" I asked.

He nodded.

"Were Mom and Dad raising their voices at each other?" I asked.

He nodded again.

I sat down on his bed and tried my best to promise him that things would work out. Gabe started to make engine noises as he played with his trucks. I left my brother's room that night wondering if I should have told him the truth. Maybe I should have told him that I just wasn't sure about anything anymore. Maybe he felt the same way.

When I walked into my bedroom, I noticed an envelope on my desk. I opened it and read the letter inside:

Dear Angel,

Hey! What's up, Angel-cake? I just wanted to wish you luck before the big race. I know how important it is to you. I'll be the loud one cheering my head off for you on the sideline. Sorry if I embarrass you. But I've always got to root for my girls.

I know you've been through a lot lately. I'm only going to write this note once because I've got a ton of homework to do. So if it all comes out funny, you'll have to forgive me.

I've got a friend at school. Her name is Peaches. Her little brother is in a wheelchair and she's never met her father. They call her Peaches because she's always smiling and always sweet. I think about my mother sometimes when I'm with Peaches. I'm thankful that I had my mother for 10 years, and that I still have my dad. I guess what I'm trying to say is that if Peaches can walk around with a smile on her face, and get through every day, then so can we.

I felt the tears well in my eyes. I had never heard Wil talk about her feelings toward her mother. I couldn't imagine how much it took for her to write this note.

> One more thing I'd thought you like. You know I don't go to church a lot and I am not the most religious person in the world. But when Penny's grandmother gave me this prayer at my mother's funeral it made me feel a little bit better. I keep it in my underwear drawer just so I see it everyday.

I laughed, which made me cry even more. Then I started reading the prayer.

One night I dreamed a dream.
I was walking along the beach with my Lord.
Across the dark sky flashed scenes from my life.
For each scene, I noticed two sets
of footprints in the sand,
one belonging to me
and one to my Lord.
When the last scene of my life shot before me
I looked back at the footprints in the sand.
There was only one set of footprints.
I realized that this was at the lowest
and saddest times of my life.
This always bothered me
and I questioned the Lord
about my dilemma.
"Lord, you told me when I decided to follow You,
You would walk and talk with me all the way.
But I'm aware that during the most troublesome
times of my life there is only one set of footprints.
I just don't understand why, when I needed You most,
You leave me."

He whispered, "My precious child,
I love you and will never leave you
never, ever, during your trials and testings.
When you saw only one set of footprints
it was then that I carried you."

We'll be cheering for you, Angel-cake!

Love,
Wil

I wiped the tears from my eyes, and lay down in my bed. Wil had given me the nicest gift in the world. I stared at the ceiling for a while and tried to make sense of all the things happening to me and my family.

After a few minutes, I stood up and walked into the bathroom. I bent over and pulled out the sack of potatoes hidden away. After staring at them for a few seconds, I pushed the unopened bag back under the sink and went back into my bedroom without my magic potatoes.

I couldn't wait to run.

Chapter Sixteen

When my eyes opened the next morning, I didn't even think about hitting the snooze button. I put my feet on the floor, rolled out of bed, fell to my knees, clasped my hands, and thanked God for allowing me to reach this special day. I stood up and dressed in my uniform. I sat on the floor and stretched my feet. I felt the pain but refused to think about it. I stood up, brushed my hair and pulled my favorite Ballplayer blue and white bow out of my drawer. I neatly tied the bow in my hair. I couldn't wait to run.

"Mom just called," my sister said as I walked into the kitchen. "She's coming over. We're all going with you."

I smiled and felt the butterflies flutter in my stomach. On any other day, I would have been stressed over my parents not being together. I forced myself to put it all out of my mind that day.

After breakfast, Gabe told me to look outside. I skipped down my front steps and read all the colorful signs that my friends had posted on our railing.

Then I felt a severe shot of pain in the arch of my right foot. *Be strong, Angel! Be strong!* There was no way my feet could fail me now. I felt another shot of pain. I stopped and stretched. After a few minutes, slowly the pain faded away.

On the way to the course, my mother and father argued over whom we would see to counsel our family that week.

"I think we should see a family social worker," my mother said.

"Reverend James will do just fine," my father insisted.

I looked at my sister. "Don't listen to them," Faith whispered. "Today is your day."

I stared out the window and blocked all the noise out of my mind. When we arrived at the course, I said good-bye to my family and jumped out of the car.

"Good luck," Faith said. "I know you can do it."

As I started to jog away, I turned back and smiled at my sister. Gabe sprinted up next to me and wrapped his arms around my waist. I almost tripped over him.

"Good luck," he said and he held on tight.

"Gabe," I said. "Please let go."

"I wish I could run with you," he said.

"I've got to run this myself," I told him.

He finally let go. I jogged up to my team and stopped right in front of Becky.

"Hey," I said. "Are you ready to do this?"

She nodded and then focused her eyes in the distance. I could see by her icy stare that Becky was already in her own zone of concentration. I sat down with Trina and Colleen and we all started to stretch.

After a few silent seconds, Colleen asked, "Are you nervous?"

She looked at Trina and me. Trina and I looked at each other. I shrugged and then Trina blurted out, "Heck, yeah. I'm a wreck!"

We all laughed. Coach Kris walked over to us and said, "Let it all go out there today. Have some fun!"

Later after our warm-up jog, I went off to the side and stretched by myself. When I felt heavy throbs of pain in my feet, I kept stretching. *Finish in the Top 20. That's all. You can do it.*

"The course is a little wet in some spots," Coach Kris announced. "Watch for the puddles."

I thought about the bends, the curves and the Mountain. Now we had to deal with soggy running shoes, too.

"You're ready for this, Angel," Coach Kris said. "You can do it. Strong and steady. Take it one step at a time."

I nodded my head. Then I sat down and laid flat on my back. I felt the moist ground under me. I closed my eyes and took deep breaths. I opened my eyes and stared into the bright blue skies above me. My body felt light. I felt strong.

As I took my position on the starting line with the rest of the runners, I heard a voice call out my name.

"You go, Angel-cake!"

I looked up and saw Wil smiling. Penny, Molly and Rosie waved. Then I stared at my mother. She winked at me. I looked at my father, surprised to see him standing right next to my mother. He grinned. Faith smiled and Gabe jumped up and down.

"Come on, Angel!" he screamed. "You can do it!"

"Runners take your mark," the starter called out over the crowd.

My thighs felt weak. A chill shot up my spine.

"Set," the starter added.

My stomach muscles twisted in a knot.

Bang! The crowd moved ferociously ahead. I couldn't believe the speed. So much for strong and steady. I felt weak and wobbly. I kept my eyes on Becky and Maura who were five feet in front of me. Then I started to lose my position. I dropped further behind. Runners passed me on the right and left. *Be strong, Angel! Be strong!* I dug my tired, sore feet into the dirt. I regained my steady stride and paced my breathing. A half-a-mile later, I regained my position. I moved right up next to Maura.

I looked up in the distance and picked a point. It was Becky White's back. Then I picked another point. The big oak tree just around the bend. It would be there that I wanted to be shoulder to shoulder with our team leader.

I moved up behind one runner just as I ran through a puddle. The mud from her shoes flung up and smacked me in the face. This ticked me off, but I didn't waste any time trying to wipe the mud from my face. I simply moved to the right and zoomed past the girl.

By this time, I had left Maura far behind. I moved closer to Becky and watched her carefully. I could tell by her wobbly stride that she was running out of gas. I ran up next to her and could hear her panting and groaning. She clutched her side and leaned forward. Fear shot up my spine. Becky White was crumbling fast. My eyes grew wide in disbelief. Becky couldn't fall apart after how much she worked. This was way too important to her.

I sucked in air for a few seconds until I felt strong enough to speak.

"Let's go," I gasped.

As we turned the bend, Becky pulled herself together and continued to match me stride for stride. When three runners passed us, I picked it up a pace, and so did Becky. I tried counting all of the runners in front of us hoping I was somewhere in the top 20, but I kept losing track. Two others sprinted by me. One ran through a mud puddle and kicked dirt in Becky's face. "Ugh!" she moaned.

I looked at the mountain. *Be strong!* I dug deep and used every ounce of energy I had. My thighs burned, and my feet throbbed. My chest ached from breathing so hard. Becky started to fall further behind me and then disappeared from my sight as I worked my way up the hill. With strong and steady strides, I made it up to the top. I picked my next point: the embankment. I gained some speed and jumped over it. By this time, I had no idea where Becky was. All I could see was the finish line.

I rounded the bend, and pumped my arms. I felt like I was stepping on broken glass with every step I took. I looked to the finish line and couldn't hear anyone. Everything started to go blurry. Then I heard a weak, raspy voice.

"Bring it in, Angel."

I saw Becky out of the corner of my eye. Slowly she moved one step ahead of me. Then two. I gritted my teeth and pushed off the ground with all of my might.

Five seconds later, it was over. Becky had beat me to my point. My whole body felt numb. I fell to the ground and started to cry. My mother and father ran up to me and grabbed me under my arms. Seeing both of them pull me up off my feet made me cry even more.

"Come on, Angel," my mother said. "Be strong."

I heard Gabe yelling, "What's the matter? What's wrong with Angel?" Then he began to cry. Coach Kris was talking to me, but I couldn't hear her. My blurry sight stopped on Wil. She looked at me in shock. There in front of all of my friends, I was a sobbing wreck. A total basket case. I straightened myself up and thought about dignity and respect. I looked up to the sky and thanked God that it was over.

"You did it!" Coach Kris yelled. "You did it!"

I finally heard what she had been trying to tell me. My eyes grew wide. "I did?" I asked in disbelief.

"You finished 20th!" she said and she patted me on the back. I just stood in shock. Gabe ran up to me and almost tackled me with his hug. Then he started crying all over again.

"I'm OK," I said. "I'm sorry I scared you."

Faith walked up to me and hugged me. "I knew you could do it!" she said. I could see the tears in her eyes.

"I'm sorry for making you cry," I said.

She wiped her tears. "I'm crying because I'm happy," she said and then she burst out laughing.

Once I felt my legs under me again, I stopped leaning on my mother and father and started to walk on my own. My feet burned with pain, and I started to limp. The slower I walked the more they hurt. Faith walked up to me and grabbed me by the side. When Trina and Colleen crossed the finish line, I cheered for them. They jogged back to the end of the stretch. My sister stood next to me as I limped over and grabbed Trina before her legs gave out.

"Thank you!" Trina said. Colleen ducked under Trina's left shoulder and held her up. "You two are the best teammates I've ever had," Trina added.

We all started to cry. A few seconds passed and Wil came up to me and said, "You can see why I don't run. It's way too emotional."

I laughed and gave her a hug. "Thanks," I said.

Then I felt a tap on my shoulder. I turned around and saw Becky White's straight face and glassy eyes. She stuck her palm out and smiled. I opened my arms and gave her a hug. Without hesitation, she hugged me back.

"Not bad for a freshman with messed up feet," she muttered.

I smiled and said, "Thanks." I could tell her body hurt by the way she hobbled over to a man who looked like her father. Becky had run the most miserable run of her life, and still came out ahead of me. It once seemed that the perfect dream would have been for me to have beaten Becky in my most important race of the year. But at the end of that race, whether Becky was in front of me or behind me didn't matter. I had picked my destination and reached that point. I had qualified for regionals. I couldn't wait to run.

But within 24 hours, everything would spin completely out of my control.

Chapter Seventeen

I started to cry the second I woke up the next morning. I flexed my leg muscles and felt the pain rip through my feet. I curled up in a ball and started to cry harder.

"It's late, Angel," Faith said. "Get up!"

I hid my face under my pillow and did not move. Then I felt a tug on my sheets. Faith pulled the cover down and looked at me in shock.

"What's wrong?" she asked.

I started crying harder. My sister ran out of the room. A few seconds later, my father came running in.

"What's the matter?" he asked.

"I can't take it anymore," I said.

He didn't ask what I was talking about and neither did Faith. They both knew what I had put myself through.

"Let's soak your feet in the tub," my father said.

My sister and father took me under each arm and helped me into the bathroom. I stared down at the steamy water and cried even more.

I insisted upon going to church with my family that morning, but my father told me it was out of the question. With a heating pad wrapped around my feet in my bed, I read the Bible all by myself.

Then I took Wil's letter out and read it over and over. The words gave me comfort, but the pain in my feet still made me sad.

The next morning, my mother took me to see Dr. Taylor. When Dr. Taylor walked into the room, I couldn't even look at her.

"You're a tough one, Angel," she said. "You made it farther than most."

I stared at the floor.

"It's not your fault," Dr. Taylor said. "You just need some rest."

"What about regionals?" I asked.

"Do you think you can run?" she asked.

I wanted so badly to nod my head, but I just sat there. My heart was telling me to be strong and run. I didn't want to disappoint Coach Kris, Trina and Colleen and all the other people who believed in me.

"Think about what you want to do," Dr. Taylor said. "You'll make the right decision."

• • • •

Wednesday morning I limped into the kitchen, picked up the phone and called my mother.

"What's the matter?" she asked.

"I'm not going to run," I said as I started to cry. "I can't."

"That's OK," she said.

"Are you disappointed in me?" I asked.

"No, honey," she said. "We're so proud of you."

"I just can't do it," I said.

"I know," she added. "It's all right. It's better that you take time off. You need your feet for a long time."

I told my father the bad news at breakfast that morning, and he gave me a hug.

"Give this time and you will heal," he said.

After school I didn't go to the pool and I didn't ride the bike. Instead I went straight to Coach Kris's office. I knocked gently on the open door. Coach Kris looked up from her desk as I walked into the room.

"I can't run," I told her.

"I know you can't," Coach Kris said.

I looked at her wondering how she knew.

"You needed to accept it," she said. "I'm glad that you finally did."

Coach Kris patted me on the back and told me to take care of myself for next year. I nodded my head and tried to smile, but deep inside I was still hurting. I went into the locker room and cleared out my belongings.

• • • •

My family started going to counseling that week, but things didn't change for the better. No matter how much I prayed, I couldn't make everything go back to the way it used to be.

On the day before regionals, Trina and Colleen asked me if I was going with the team to watch Becky run. I really didn't want to go. I talked things over with Faith that night, and we both agreed that I was being selfish. I made myself go for Becky.

As I stood on the sidelines, I watched the pack of runners and felt every high and low they felt as they ran their exhausted bodies through the difficult course. In the end, some collapsed, some cried, others laughed and smiled. They all finished.

Becky ran the best race of her life and qualified for states. Before I left that day, Becky came up to me and said, "Thanks."

I nodded thinking that she was thanking me for coming out to watch her run.

"I won't forget how you helped me," she said. "We carried each other."

On the drive home, we drove by Anderson Park. I looked up in the distance and saw Gabe playing on the swings. I glanced around for my mother and father or some of Gabe's friends. Some high school kids walked down the sidewalk and three kids shot baskets on the court. Gabe was all by himself.

"Can you let me out here please?" I asked Trina's mother.

I thanked Trina and her mother for the ride and said good-bye. I took a few steps down the sidewalk and I heard a voice call my name. I turned around. It was Faith. I stopped and waited until she caught up to me.

"Hi," I said. "What are you doing?"

"I'm going to get Gabe," she said.

"So am I," I said. "I don't know how many times we have to tell him not to come down to the park all by himself."

As Faith and I walked closer to Gabe, I watched him run around the playground. He gritted his teeth as he hung from the monkey bars. He winced after he jumped and landed on his feet. Then he smiled as he slid down the slippery slide. Finally he turned to us.

"Hi!" he said with a big smile.

"What are you doing down here all alone?" I asked.

"I am not alone," Gabe said.

I glanced around and said, "Yes, you are."

"No, I'm not!" Gabe shot back.

"There's nobody here with you."

"Yes there is!" he insisted.

"Who?" I asked.

"You and Faith," he said.

About the Author

In writing this series, I have spent a lot of time thinking about my family, especially my brothers and sister.

When I was growing up, I used to always want to play sports with my older brother Kevin and his friends. As much as the boys at school razzed Kevin for having a sister who could play ball, he never held a grudge. Everyone always asked him if I could beat him in a game of one-on-one. The few times that Kevin and I played, we didn't keep score. Something else was more important than points. When kids asked Kevin about me, I had heard that he always told them how hard I worked. That meant more to me than any victory.

Kevin is a police officer now. Whenever people ask me about him, I always tell them how hard he works and how great he is at what he does.

My younger brother Ryan plays basketball in college. Over the years, we've been pretty tough on each other. When we were kids, our games of one-on-one in the driveway usually ended with somebody in tears.

Now during the summer, Ryan plays in a few basketball leagues. For some games, Ryan's team doesn't have enough players. If I'm home, Ryan always asks me to play before anyone else. One night last summer Ryan had a game. His team had enough players, so I decided to stay home and write. Ryan didn't talk to me for days. I didn't realize how much it meant to him for me to be there.

My younger sister Meghan is my toughest editor and my best friend. Meg plays basketball in college, too. My mother never liked us to go up to the gym alone, so I always talked my sister into coming with me. I took Meg up to the gym with me for hours on end. I used to play these games against myself where I had to make so many shots before we could leave. As the ball bounced off the rim and around the gym, Meg grew tired and cranky. But she never left me until I finished what I had started. Now when I visit Meg at her college, we always stop by the gym to shoot baskets. I never leave Meg until she reaches her goal.

I carry these feelings for my brothers and sister with me no matter where I go or what I do.

In your hands is my fourth book.

Check out the rest of the books written by

Broadway

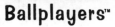

Ballplayers™

Book # 1
Friday Nights
by Molly

Molly O'Malley loves basketball and she can't stand to lose. At the start of the first city summer league, Molly only thinks about winning the championship, but the Ballplayers run into some serious competition both on and off the court. Will the Ballplayers be the team to bring the championship to Broadway?

Book # 2
Left Out
by Rosie

Rosie Jones is one of the best 11-year old baseball players in the city. But will she make the all-star team? No matter how hard she works, will Rosie ever be good enough for her father?

PLAY WITH PASSION!

Book # 3
Everybody's Favorite
by Penny

When Penny Harris finds out the Ballplayers have a chance to go to soccer camp, she can't wait. But there's only one catch — they have to raise all the money in one week. Along the way, the Ballplayers run into trouble, and everyone looks to one person to save the day. Will Penny be able to work everything out?

Book #5
Sideline Blues
by Wil

Back in third and fourth grade, Wil Thomas was one of the best athletes in her class, but now all of her teammates have caught up with her. Even though Wil tries her best, she is seeing less playing time in her volleyball games. Some teachers tell Wil not worry about sports and to concentrate on school, but she wants to play. What is Wil going to do?

More books on the way?
Let us know if you want to read more about
The Broadway Ballplayers™

Join the Ballplayer Book Club!

Get your T-Shirt, pens, pencils, bookmark, whistle key chain, bag, and newsletter.

Complete Book Club: $30
Book Club (T-shirt only): $15

Ballplayer Name _____

Age _____

Street Address _____

City/State/Zip _____

❏ Please charge my credit card $ _____

    ❏ MasterCard   ❏Visa

    No. _____ Exp. Date _____

    Signature _____

❏ Enclosed is my check for $ _____

❏ Navy blue T-Shirt   Size S M L XL XXL

To join the Book Club or to simply add your name to the mailing list, send form or a note to:

Ballplayer Headquarters
P.O. Box 597
Wilmette, IL 60091
(847) 570-4715

THE Broadway

Ballplayers™

www.bplayers.com

E-mail author Maureen Holohan
at maureen@bplayers.com